SLAPSHOT

Slapshot

REBECCA JENSHAK

HeartEyes Press

This book was inspired by the True North Series written by Sarina Bowen. It is an original work that is published by Heart Eyes Press LLC.

KAITLYN

Living in the dorms as a junior is torture. There's the cramped closet, the shared bathroom, ancient furniture, and dingy walls. And, of course, the total lack of privacy.

It's especially terrible when you've already lived on your own and know the joys of independence and a quality mattress. All those things would be reason enough to miss my old life, complete with apartment, but I also have a roommate issue. An awful, unspeakable, truly shocking roommate issue.

She's sleeping with my ex-boyfriend.

Listening to your ex have sex with anyone else, let alone your roommate, should be grounds for a transfer to another room.

It isn't. I checked.

My RA was very understanding. She used those exact words several times. *"I completely understand."* And then she suggested ear plugs or sitting down with my roommate and having an honest conversation about how I was feeling.

A decent suggestion if I had any desire to speak to my ex-boyfriend's new girlfriend. I do not need to add humiliation to the long list of emotions the situation has thrown at me. Anger, sadness, jealousy, to name a few. Moo U was supposed to be a fresh start, not more lessons on coping with heartbreak.

"How long are they going to keep that up?" my friend Vivian asks with an impressed smile on her pink, glossy lips. She sits on my bed, staring at the wall separating mine and Chastity's bedrooms.

"Judging by the moans, we have another few minutes until they finish." I don't look up from my laptop where I read through my notes for my content marketing class. We have a test tomorrow, and I am struggling to focus.

"I don't know whether to be disgusted or turned on. Are they always this loud?"

"Disgusted and *always*."

And here comes the name calling.

"Dylan. Oh, Dylan."

This is when I usually blast my music to drown them out. I could almost pretend it was someone else if it weren't for the talking. Is it too much to ask that they do it at his place? Or use a ball gag?

There may be a wall between us, but a floor, or twelve, wouldn't be enough. Last week I caught a glimpse of Dylan, my now ex, coming out of the shower naked. He's not at all hard to look at, and it just made me angry and sad all over again about how things went down between us.

When I got to Burlington University, not so affectionately known as *Moo U* for the bull mascot, I thought it was a stroke of good luck that I got paired with Chastity as a roommate.

We have absolutely nothing in common, but her hunky best friend was the first look of something good I'd had since I was kicked out of my last college and shipped off to freaking Vermont.

Turns out he was a mirage, and I was too tired and thirsty from crawling through hell to realize it until he was breaking promises and running off for long weekends to hang with his *friend* Chastity. I've learned the hard way that you can't rely on things that seem too good to be true.

"Wow. You'd think with the wall between you, it'd muffle it somewhat. But it's like they're in the room," Vivian whispers. I don't know why. They obviously aren't worried about people overhearing. "I think I can hear him spanking her ass."

"She's slapping the wall," I supply. It super annoys me that I know their whole sex routine. They don't vary it up much—though they sound utterly content refining the one routine. A perfect ten from both judges if I'm going by the screaming orgasm followed by silence.

"Lunch and a show. I think I need a jolt of caffeine after that. Do you want to hit the coffee shop before class?"

"Please. I can't listen to any more of that."

"There's more?"

"Give it five minutes."

"I'm sorry," Vivian catches herself. "That has to be awful. You know you're welcome to crash at my place any time."

"Thank you. I'll survive." Whatever this year throws at me, and it's thrown a lot, I will manage. There's no other option.

I tuck my laptop into my backpack, and we trek from my dorm to the student union on the other side of campus. For all the ways my time at Moo U has been disappointing, the campus has exceeded my expectations.

My last college in New York was all money and prestige. Just one of many colleges in a big city. Tall buildings crammed together so close to others that it was hard to tell where one campus ended, and another began.

Here, the university is the heart of the city and it shows in every detail. Lush grounds, buildings spread out with room to walk or sit outside. The Vermont scenery is a pleasant addition, too. Fall is here. The leaves have changed and it's that perfect time of year when you forget how brutal the coming winter months will be and just get lost in the picturesque beauty of it.

I breathe it all in. When life hands you lemons, you make lemonade. When it throws Vermont at you, you put on your favorite boots and admire the scenery.

The Green Bean, the campus coffeehouse, is packed. We stand at the back of the line to wait our turn. Everyone around us is wearing Burlington University green to support the hockey team. They play Michigan tomorrow night. It really pains me to know so much about a sport I despise, but Moo U hockey is a really big deal. I should know, my dad was one of their biggest stars twenty-some years ago.

"What are we doing tonight?" my best friend asks.

Usually by Thursday, we've already planned our entire weekend, but since hockey season started the options are dwindling. Moo U is a hockey school. When students enroll, they're given a schedule of games and a Moo U Hockey bumper sticker with their welcome packet.

The hockey players are gods, and their games are like giant parties for the student body. Or that's what I hear. I haven't actually been. Nor do I intend to go.

"We could go out, grab dinner, hit the poetry slam, and then the bars," she suggests.

"Why bother? It'll be dead tonight while everyone rests up for tomorrow night's game."

"Not everyone. There has to be some cute guys in this town that don't care about hockey."

I glance behind us into the sea of green. "Have you looked around? The game isn't until tomorrow and they're already pumped to watch them destroy Michigan."

We laugh together and then it's our turn at the counter. Vivian orders her usual—skinny cinnamon dolce latte. I peruse the menu. I'm working my way through every flavor and variation to find my favorite. When I was in New York, I was just like Vivian. Always ordering the same thing. My favorite drink was the iced ginger coconut milk. It's not the same here. Nothing is.

I haven't found my favorite anything in Vermont yet.

"And for you?" the barista asks before I've decided.

"I don't know. Surprise me. But not what she ordered." I make a face as I remember the horrid taste of Vivian's favorite drink.

"Today's special is the puck drop." She leans closer. "It's just a hot mocha, but it has green whipped cream." Her eyes widen and she flashes me a big smile. "Go Bulls!"

I feel my brows raise, but I manage to keep my snarky thoughts to myself. "Sure, the puck drop sounds fine, but no whipped cream."

She gives me the total and I hand her my debit card.

"Where's your team spirit?" Vivian asks with an eye roll.

"The same place yours went."

"I'm sorry." The barista holds up my card with a sympathetic look. "It's not going through."

The card swiper machine is on the counter between us.

"There must be a mistake. Let me try." I insert my card and an uneasy feeling settles over me as the word *Declined* appears on the screen.

"That's weird," I say awkwardly to the barista as I start to sweat.

"What's wrong?" Vivian grabs her drink from the counter.

"My card was declined."

"Maybe it was stolen, and the bank put a freeze on it."

"Maybe." Though as I say it, I don't believe it. I know I've been cutting it close lately, but I didn't think it was quite this dire.

Vivian uses her card to pay for my drink and we walk to our classes together. She chats away about what she's going to wear tonight and how she hopes she meets a cute guy. I'm only half listening. That uneasy feeling from earlier has turned into a pit of doom as I scroll through the many purchases on my bank account card. Coffee, coffee, nails, boots… I really should have been more careful, but I didn't really believe my dad when he said that he wasn't giving me any more money this semester. I thought he was bluffing, but apparently not. And I'll starve before calling and telling him I'm broke.

Oh my god, I'm broke.

"So, you'll come by later and we'll pick outfits and get all glammed up?" she asks when we get to her art class building.

"Sure."

"Sure? Wow, well, don't get too excited about a night out or anything." She hip checks me playfully.

I tuck my phone back into my pocket. "I'm sorry. I was thinking about my card. I need to get it straightened out. Can we go out tomorrow night instead?"

"Of course. I suppose I could study for my art history test next week." She makes a face. "Do you want me to come with you to the bank after class? Those people can be scary talking about account closures and fees." She shudders. I wonder if she's speaking from experience. The way she spends money, I can very well see how she might reach the end of even a very high credit limit. I don't really blame her. When people give you everything you want, you start to expect it.

"Thank you, but no, I've got this. I have to go somewhere even scarier than the bank to settle this."

"Scarier than the bank?" she squeaks.

"Way scarier."

On the second floor of the student employment office, a woman named Holly ushers me into a seat in front of her messy desk. It's lined with pictures of small dogs wearing sweaters and cheesy costumes.

I hand her my resume, and she sets it on top of a pile of papers without glancing at it.

"Well, most of the campus jobs have already been filled for the semester, but here's what I have." She places a finger on her monitor and slides it across the screen as she says, "Spanish tutor, dining services attendant, and they're looking for an aide in the early childhood education center." She looks to me hopefully.

Unless I can learn Spanish overnight, that's out.

Hair net? Absolutely not.

"I was hoping for something in marketing. That's my major and I'm applying for this super competitive internship next summer and could use some relatable experience on my resume." Maybe if I look at this as experience instead of desperation, I can put a happy spin on it.

But Holly does not look like she cares about my hopes and dreams. That would make her one of many.

And I'm out of options unless I want to take a chance that one of the restaurants or bars in Burlington are hiring a girl with no experience at… well, anything.

With a sigh, I ask, "What does an aide do in the education center? Teach colors and play games with the kids?"

"This position is more diapering and sanitizing than teaching. We have actual teachers for the older kids. You'd be working alongside the lead teacher of the infant room doing whatever they need to keep the little ones safe and entertained." She scrunches up her nose.

Something tells me by the lack of baby photos on her desk

and the disgusted look on her face, Holly and I are on the same page about changing diapers. Eww.

"There's nothing else?"

"I'm sorry. This far into the semester..." She trails on, lecturing me about all the good jobs being snatched up quickly and how I should have started my search earlier. I sit back and take it. I've gotten impressively good at zoning out when adults lecture me.

Mostly from my dad.

You've been given a chance to start over. Use it wisely. No more games. No more blowing off classes and letting your grades fall. In fact, I'm not adding any more money to your account until I see your first semester grades. Essentials only. I'm serious, Kaitlyn. Last chance to get it together.

I really hadn't thought he was serious. I've had nearly unlimited funds since I was sixteen. You can't just cut someone off like that. And I have been doing better with my spending. Last week I bought a pair of boots from the half-off rack. If I'd known the boots were the last purchase I'd be able to make for a while, I might have done things differently. Too late now.

"Oh wait." Her voice lifts three octaves, snapping me back to her droning speech. "A new job just posted. It's with the athletic department. The hockey team is looking for an equipment manager."

"Girls' or boys' team?"

I already know it's too much to assume it'd be the girls' team. That is not the type of year I'm having.

"The boys' team. If you're interested, I'd hustle over. It will not stay vacant for long. Would you like me to call Coach Keller and get more information?" She looks so damn optimistic. I guess if your job is hooking people up with employment, this is the moment you live for. Unfortunately for her, I have a long track record of disappointing people.

"No." I stand. "I think I'll try off-campus jobs."

Not today, Satan.

"You're sure? It's one of the best paid student jobs at the university." She adjusts her monitor to show me the hourly pay, all with a smile like she's found me the golden ticket.

My stomach sinks at the number.

So that's the cost of selling your soul.

LEX

"Is that a smile on his face?" Tate whispers. We're standing in the back of the group as Coach Keller gives the team a few last-minute words of encouragement for tomorrow's game.

I huff out a quiet laugh and nod. "Freaky, right?"

We're coming off two back-to-back winning weekends and another great week of practice. Everyone is in good spirits. Even our hard-ass coach, who isn't known for his sunny disposition, looks happy. Or is attempting to. His smile somehow makes him look scarier.

I think I'm the only one that isn't walking on air, dreaming of an undefeated record, and holding that Frozen Four trophy overhead.

It's hard to be optimistic about your awesome team when you're the suckiest part of it.

"Nice work today, boys. See you tomorrow," Coach dismisses us. "Vonne, hang back for a minute."

Tate shoots me a pitying look before he and the rest of the guys head off to the locker room. I skate over to Coach Keller. That hint of a smile he had when addressing the whole team is gone as he leans on a hockey stick and regards me.

"I'm going to move you to the left wing with Scoville and Thomas. You're the fastest skater on the team. Maybe that I've ever coached. I think your speed will give us a nice boost on that fourth line."

All the praise bounces off me and the words fourth line echo in my head. *Fourth line.*

It might as well be Siberia. Our fourth line gets the least amount of ice time. I'm struggling to find my footing with the team, but I'm better than fourth line. The only real expectation of those guys is not to screw anything up. Give the top lines a rest and maybe get a few good hits in.

I'm not that guy—the one you expect nothing from. I was the leading scorer of my high school team, I was named first team all-state, I had my choice of hockey colleges. Moo U wasn't even the best offer I received. Partial scholarship instead of the full-ride that had been dangled in front of me by a dozen other schools. But Burlington University is one of the best. Maybe the best. Coach Keller is a legend.

"Coach, I just need a little more time to adjust. Please, don't move me yet." I've got my eye on the second line. I *need* that second line. Not just because it means more playing time and more opportunities on the ice, it says my hard work has finally paid off and I've made it.

His mouth pulls into a thin line.

I try to keep going, make him hear me out. Just another few games before he gives up on me. "I've been working with Pax—"

My protest is cut short when our assistant coach, Coach Garfunkle, calls across the ice, "Coach, our next interview is here."

He stands on the edge of the ice next to a girl with long, brown hair. Through my frustration, I take in her short blue dress and over-the-knee boots. Her cherry red lips are full and pouty. Eyes downcast, she holds a coffee, looking like she'd rather be anywhere else.

There's a stiffness to her body and the way she holds herself that refuses to make her look weak, just highly disinterested or put out.

That makes two of us. She's cutting short my time with Coach to make a case, grovel, or beg, because I'm not above that. Hockey is everything. I didn't move across the country to watch my really great team win hockey games. I came to be a part of that.

Coach Keller glances over and then nods and stands straight. "Let's see how it goes this weekend and we can make more adjustments if needed. See you tomorrow, Vonne."

I make my way to the locker room slowly. The noise gets louder with every step. The boys are joking, laughing, making plans to go to the Biscuit for wings and a couple of beers. We have a game tomorrow so it'll be an early night. Someone is singing, loudly and off-key in the showers as I get inside.

I peel off my practice jersey and slump onto the bench next to Tate. He shoots me a worried look, but he won't ask in front of everyone else.

Patrick is talking from his other side. "She's hot. Kind of a train wreck, but still smoking hot."

"Why is she a train wreck? Because she likes to drink and make-out at parties?" Tate asks and raises a brow. "Sound familiar?"

Patrick grins. He's a hell of a hockey player and a hell of a partier. Somehow, he manages to juggle both. "You're right, she's the girl version of me. Maybe I should ask her out."

"Now that sounds like a train wreck," Patrick's twin brother, Paxton, the saner of the two says. "What do you think she's doing here?"

"Checking up on daddy's investment probably." Patrick holds up a skate.

"Did you hear anything, Vonne?" Paxton asks.

"What?" I glance up and then process their conversation. "Nah."

"Him?" Patrick points the skate in his hand toward me now. "He doesn't see chicks, only hockey."

Tate folds his arms over his chest. "Yeah, but she's hockey royalty, so I think it's a gray area."

"Verdict?" Paxton prompts and the three of them look to me expectantly.

"What the hell are you guys talking about?" My mind is still spinning with disappointment from being demoted.

Patrick groans. "Rook, you're killing me."

"Kaitlyn Dalager was talking with Coach Garfunkle at the end of practice."

"Okay. So?"

"Kaitlyn Dalager," Patrick says slowly, like it should mean something.

"Am I supposed to know who that is?" An image of the pretty girl I saw a few minutes ago flashes in my head. I'm positive I've never seen her before. She's the kind of girl you remember.

"Declan Dalager. He played for the Bruins, owns Dalager Sports."

There's a groan that I'm pretty sure comes from Patrick.

"He's alum of the university. His senior year Moo U won the Frozen Four and then the next year, his rookie season with the Bruins he won the Stanley Cup," Paxton adds. "His daughter Kaitlyn transferred here this year as a junior."

"Right, yeah, his name is everywhere." And it really is. Trophies and jerseys, plaques. That's the kind of legacy I want to leave behind.

"I heard she got kicked out of her last college," Tate says, voice lowered.

Patrick snorts. "I heard she was sleeping with a married professor and the wife found out."

"I wonder what her dad thought of that," Paxton says with a contemplative stare.

All their chattering is hurting my already pounding head. Who the hell cares?

I picked up hockey later than most of these guys. I was playing football with absolutely no desire to touch any other sport when my parents split, and my mom moved to Minnesota. My brother and I decided to stay in Arizona for the school year, which meant summers we had to spend a month away from our friends sitting in her apartment with no friends and nothing to do.

What started as something to keep us occupied, camps and then pickup games with guys we met, turned into an obsession for me. I quit football altogether my senior year to focus solely on hockey.

The twins are dressed and ready to go first. My limbs are heavy and I'm sluggish. I'm not really in the mood to drink and kick back. I don't have time for a pity party. I need to figure out how to fix this and do it. Fast.

"Meet you guys at the Biscuit?" Paxton asks me and Tate.

"Yeah." I nod my agreement. "Tate, can I get a ride?"

Tate runs a hand through his wet hair. "Sure thing."

"Oh, *you're* actually coming, Adler?" Patrick mocks with a smirk. "No romantic dates planned with Maggie tonight?"

Tate's mouth pulls into a smug smile. "She's meeting us there."

We're all still trying to get used to Tate having a girlfriend. Maggie is cool though.

When they're gone, Tate sits to wait for me. "What'd Coach say?"

The locker room is still loud, and no one is paying us any mind, but I glance around before answering. "He's switching me and Roddy."

The implication of that hits him immediately and he grimaces. "Shit, Lex, I'm sorry."

"It's fine. It's fine," I mumble, mostly trying to convince myself. "I'm playing like shit. I'm lucky he hasn't taken me out altogether."

"You're not playing like shit," he starts, but I level him with a look that calls bull. "Okay, you're struggling a bit. You have to find your place on the team, get a groove playing with the guys instead of doing it all. You came from a team where you were the hotshot and you needed to do it all. Now you're on a team with some of the best college hockey players in the country and you just need to be part of a bigger puzzle. You'll get there. You'll find your place."

Hopefully that place isn't on the fourth line. Maybe I'm expecting too much as a freshman.

I couldn't be the star player here even if I wanted to. Some of these guys are just straight better than I am. Paxton Graham, for starters. He's already been drafted to play professionally. The guy is a total powerhouse on our first line. Patrick may be the one people talk about when they mention the Graham twins, but Paxton has this quiet presence that I find really admirable. Plus, he has a wicked slapshot.

I don't expect to be the team's star player, but I want to contribute. I want to feel like I'm adding value. I've got my eye on that second line and I know I'm capable of getting there.

"Maybe I should skip the Biscuit, stay and work some drills." I bet I could text Pax and he'd come back to help me.

Work harder. It's a motto that's served me well. In hockey and in life.

"There's more to life than hockey." Tate stands. "Come on, first round is on me."

3

KAITLYN

"How's your father?" Coach Keller grins from behind his desk and laces his fingers at his waist. I should have expected this, but it still stings.

I get this a lot. People give me their full attention, but only because they're interested in knowing what the great Declan Dalager is up to.

Running a freshly manicured finger along the rim of the coffee lid, I force a smile. I probably should have dumped the coffee before my meeting with Holly or before coming straight here afterward, but if it's the last one I'm going to have for a while, I'm going to enjoy every last drop.

"Great. He's really good."

"I haven't seen him since they inducted him into the school's Hall of Fame. Guess that was almost ten years ago. Now that you're here, I bet we'll see a lot more of him."

I wouldn't count on it.

Still smiling, I nod. "So, the job..."

"Right, right." He sits forward. "Well, our last equipment manager dropped out of school and left a heap of dirty laundry for me to deal with. The freshmen have been rotating turns and you can guess how much they enjoy that." He chuckles. "It's not all laundry, as I'm sure you know. Sharpening skates, prepping practices and games, making repairs to gear when needed. Coach Garfunkle does the ordering but taking inventory and letting him know when we're running low is also something that our past EMs have done."

"Sounds easy enough."

"Well, some of the guys are pretty particular about their gear, but I'm sure you understand that. Your dad re-taped his stick before every period without fail." He grins like we're sharing some inside joke.

I was five when my dad retired from the NHL. I've seen video, of course, and heard countless stories, but details like that—are little gems. I'd love to ask him to tell me more about my dad's pregame routines, but I don't want to let on like I didn't already know either.

My dad stopped sharing those types of tidbits when I quit hockey at thirteen and told him I never wanted to step foot on the ice again. I guess you could say he's been eternally disappointed in me since then.

"Well, I would love to be considered for the job. I emailed over my resume. I know that I don't have experience, but I am a quick learner."

"It's yours if you want it." He waves a hand.

"Really?" And here I was prepared to list all the reasons that I'd be a great employee. Okay, fine, there's only one reason—I'm desperate.

He grins at my surprise. "You're probably the most qualified person we've ever had apply. Nearly all of our equipment is Dalager."

Right. Of course. Except the last time I was in the Dalager Sports office for something other than trying to get five minutes of face time with my dad was… so long I don't even remember.

"Great." My palms start to sweat at the realization I'm actually going through with this. It was one thing to make the appointment and show up, but am I really going to sign up for a semester of washing laundry and being the fetch girl for a team full of cocky and annoying hockey players?

"I'll have Coach Garfunkle show you around this afternoon and then tomorrow we'll need you here early to prep for our game. We've got two tough teams this weekend. It's a great time to jump right in."

"Oh, I'm sorry. I have plans." The lie slips out before I can stop it. Call it an automatic defense mechanism because holy shit is this really happening? Still, I need this job, so I try for a regretful smile. "I didn't realize the job would start immediately."

I'm going to need a day or two to let this all sink in. While I eat ramen.

Coach Keller has been around for a long time. He has an expression that's hard to read, but I'm certain he can see right through my lie. I do have plans, that isn't a lie, but I doubt he'd consider a night out with Vivian a very good excuse. He nods. "Okay. When can you start?"

I glance down at my coffee and wiggle my toes inside my new boots. If I want any semblance of my old life back, then it's this job or changing diapers. I already checked the local job listings on my way to this interview. None of the off-campus jobs come close to matching the equipment manager salary. "Is Saturday okay?"

"Great." He stands and extends a hand. "I think we can manage one more night on our own. I'll let the boys know the good news. We're excited to have you on board. Tell your father hello."

I walk out of the office on wobbly legs. So, it isn't exactly what I had in mind for my fresh start, but if all I have to do is sharpen skates and do laundry, organize equipment—things I could do in my sleep, then maybe it won't be so bad. Still, my stomach twists.

The things a girl will do for a decent cup of coffee, a killer pair of boots, and a chance to get back in her father's good graces.

"You aren't dressed to go out," Vivian says as she holds her apartment door open for me Friday night.

"I'm not going to be able to make it."

"You came all the way over here to tell me you can't go out?"

I lift the bottle of wine in my hand.

"Your emergency stash?" she questions. "This must be bad."

I walk into her cute, single bedroom apartment. "I got a job."

"A job?" Her brows pull together. I can tell she wasn't expecting this. Why would she? We both come from well-off families where money isn't an issue. "Somewhere cool? Oh, did you get that marketing internship with..." She waves her hand. "I can't remember the name of the place."

"No, that isn't until next summer. I'm interviewing with them at the career fair."

"Okay, well then where is it?" She sets out glasses and grabs a wine opener. When I don't answer, she stops and holds up a hand, exaggerating my delay. "Hello? Earth to Kaitlyn?" She goes back to opening the wine. "Please don't tell me you got a job at the dining hall. Hair nets are social suicide. No guy wants to fuck the lunch lady."

"No, I'm not... I mean it is on campus, but..."

She groans. "Oh my gosh, you're killing me. Where is it?"

"I'm the new equipment manager for the hockey team," I spit out.

You'd think I slapped her by her sharp intake of breath and the stunned look on her face. She drinks straight out of the bottle.

"But... why?" she asks after she's taken a healthy sip. "And I cannot stress this enough... WHY?"

"I need a job. My checking account is empty, and I cannot spend the rest of the year eating greasy cafeteria food. I had my coffee out of the break room in the teacher's lounge this morning." A shiver runs through me at the memory of that bitter, burned taste. I won't make that mistake again.

"I had no idea. Also, I can cover your coffee." She grabs her phone while I tell her the rest of the story.

"Thank you, but it isn't just that. My dad cut me off until he sees my semester grades and I've convinced him I'm not going to get kicked out of another university. The only way I'm going to get my dad to start depositing money again is to show him that I'm making an effort. I do not want to be the girl who has to wait until her friends offer to pay to leave the dorm. It's bad enough that I'm one of the few upperclassmen living in the dorm, I refuse to spend my weekends sitting in and waiting for a dorm social activity where I can get free punch and cookies." It feels sort of awful when I say it all out loud. I realize that's the first time I've told anyone. Even Dylan didn't get the whole story. It's super embarrassing to be a poor rich girl.

"That is the saddest story I've ever heard." She pours me a glass.

My phone pings with an incoming Venmo alert. *Vivian paid Kaitlyn. Thanks for showing me a good time, sweet thing. $100.*

"Vivian, no. Thank you, but no, I can't take money from you."

"It's just to hold you over. I'm sure I owe you for drinks or dinner, or something." She waves it off and changes the subject. "How are you going to have time to study or go out? Hold the phone, do you have to like go to the games now?"

"Yeah, that's basically the job."

"Couldn't you find something else? Hockey players are the worst and now our weekends are ruined. What about the soccer team? They're not tools and I could come with you and help."

I chuckle lightly. As if it's as easy as snapping my fingers and getting any job I want. Don't I wish. "No, they already have one. Equipment manager jobs hardly ever come available. I lucked out that the hockey team had an opening. Besides, I could do this job in my sleep."

"Sounds like a nightmare. Be careful. Don't let the sweat and pheromones make you dumb."

"I will be fine."

She tilts her head and purses her lips.

"I solemnly swear not to fall for a hockey player." I raise my hand as if I'm taking an oath.

"If you say so. Go put something on from my closet. We're going out and *I'm* paying."

"No, I don't feel up to it."

"Is this about Dylan? You can't hide from him forever."

"No. Although I did see him and Chastity on the way here."

"What'd you say?"

"Nothing, I pretended I didn't see them. They were walking ahead of me, holding hands." I hate how happy they are. No, that's not true. I hate how happy they are with zero regard for what their relationship did to me.

"The best revenge is moving on. Look at the back of my closet. That's where all the really skimpy dresses are."

"They aren't why I can't go out. I have no money."

"I've got it. If this is our last Friday night without hockey, I want to enjoy it." She winks playfully at me. Her green eyes are bright and big. Lashes coated to perfection and her lips are painted in this season's new shiny red. Vivian is always meticulously put together. Even her casual wear is expensive and trendy. She's the quintessential rich girl to everyone else. To me, she's a girl projecting one image and hiding all her insecurities. It's the number one thing we have in common. Well, that and our habit of doing exactly the opposite of what's expected of us.

"I can't believe I'm going to be working with the hockey team. This year just keeps kicking my ass." I shake my head. "I need a night in. Just the two of us and absolutely no talk of hockey."

"A night in? No way. This is your last night of freedom. Let's celebrate!"

I don't give in.

"Fine." She huffs a sigh and sticks out her bottom lip. "We will stay in, but tomorrow after the game, I'm treating you to a night on the town." She lifts her glass to cheers. "You got a job!"

I'm pretty sure she's faking her excitement, but I still love her for it. Hopefully some of that fake enthusiasm will rub off on me.

KAITLYN

Saturday morning, I meet Coach Garfunkle in the equipment room. It's down the hall but attached to the locker room. Some of the guys are already here dressing for their morning skate. They won their game against Michigan last night and today they play Northeastern University.

"How long have you been without a manager?" I ask as I take in the state of the room. It's clear there was once some concept of organization, but it looks like it was long abandoned.

"Two weeks. Alec, the last manager, had planned to be gone one of those weeks, so we didn't realize he wasn't coming back at first." He moves to a desk hidden under a pile of papers and snatches a tablet off the top. "Everything you need to know is on here. Alec created checklists for home and away games. He has information on each player's preferences, and probably a bunch of other stuff I don't know about. He was thorough, the guys on the team loved him. He really kept us up and running."

"Great. No pressure."

"I have a good feeling about you. You have a red aura. It's

dim and there's a lot of darkness surround it, but it's there." He squints his eyes and studies me. I dumbly look around myself like I expect to see colors emanating from my body.

"Thank you?" I have no idea if that's the sort of thing you thank someone for.

He keeps staring for a beat and then straightens and gives me a big, cheeky smile. He digs something out of his pocket and holds it out to me. "I almost forgot. This is for you."

I stare at the white and blue rock in his palm.

"It's a moonstone. For new beginnings and good fortune." He sets it on the desk. "We told the guys this morning. Everyone is really happy to have you here. Well, I'll let you get familiar with everything and I'll check in later. Northeastern should be arriving in about two hours. Let's set up their locker room first. I'll be around if you have any questions."

Unraveling the red scarf from my neck, I laugh as I set it on the desk. Red scarf equals red aura, I guess. He's certainly a contrast to the gruff head coach. I wonder what color is Coach Keller's aura?

I power on the tablet and find the files Coach Garfunkle mentioned. It's extensive. Player profiles, step-by-step instructions for setting up the locker rooms and packing for away games. An uneasy feeling settles in my stomach at the thought of traveling with the team. It's one thing to give up a few hours of my day but being trapped with a horde of hockey players on a bus or in a hotel somewhere isn't something I thought through. If I had, I wouldn't be here now.

I push that away to deal with later and using the checklist for game day to-dos, I go through the motions finding gear and reorganizing the stick wall.

Occasionally I notice someone standing in the doorway and turn to find one of the players walking by at a snail's pace. At least six different guys creep by to scope me out. They don't speak. No one introduces themselves, or welcomes me to the team, asks for help. I'm not sure they're as happy to have me as Coach Garfunkle let on.

I expected to be mauled and questioned as soon as they realized I was here. I once had a guy ask me to a middle school dance just so he could meet my dad. The first of many times boys have feigned interest in me to get to my dad. Maybe if they don't speak to me, this won't be so bad.

Once the guys go out for their skate, I finally relax. I fight with the sewing machine making repairs to uniforms, Coach Garfunkle drops back in and shows me how to work the skate sharpening machine, and before I know it, I'm folding towels and wiping down benches in the away team's locker room.

It's pretty mindless work, really. I'm taking a last glance around when Coach Garfunkle appears with guys from Northeastern University. Bags on shoulders, most of them wear headphones or have them resting around their necks.

"All ready?" Coach Garfunkle asks with an easy smile.

I nod and move out of the center of the room. The guys filter in while Coach Garfunkle introduces me to our opponent's equipment manager.

"This is Kaitlyn. She has you guys covered, whatever you need." Our assistant coach starts out of the locker room. I don't know why he has so much faith in me, but I appreciate that he doesn't hover trying to mansplain things to me.

"You're new." Northeastern's manager drops a bag onto the floor.

"That's right."

"Which guy do you belong to?"

"Excuse me?"

"Which guy on the team are you dating?" When I don't immediately answer, he adds, "Come on, hot chick like you. Why else would you sign up for this job? Unless you're into one of them and he doesn't know it. Maybe all of them." He shrugs as if he didn't just offend me on so many levels I can't wrap my brain around his arrogance.

He doesn't know who I am, but if he did, he'd be mortified. In some ways, I prefer his assholery. At least it's honest.

"I'm not dating any of them, nor do I want to," I say and give him my best professional smile laced with annoyance and don't fuck with me. I've worked hard on this look, but this guy just chuckles.

"Yeah, sure, okay. Do you want to give me your number and I can text you if we need anything?"

I hesitate. I don't know if that's a normal request or not. Seems reasonable, but I don't really want this prick to have my number. "I'll check in after the first period. Good luck."

Back in our locker room, the guys are getting dressed, so I prep the bench. Fans are starting to trickle into the arena, and I'm as nervous as if I were about to take the ice.

Northeastern skates out first, but Moo U is close behind. Coach Keller adjusts his tie as he steps onto the bench. I glance down at the green polo shirt that is my uniform. It's boxy and unflattering and faintly smells like body odor.

"Did you have any trouble today?" he asks.

"No, I don't think so."

"If the boys haven't complained by now, then I think you're safe." His eyes scan the area. "Looks good."

I stand back and watch the team. A funny feeling comes over me as my senses are accosted with memories. I swear the air tastes different when you're standing near the ice. The smell of the snack bar, the sound of skates gliding over the ice, and the way the overhead lights make the ice shine.

Some of the earliest pictures of me are on the ice. I guess that's why even though I've largely avoided it for the past eight years, my breathing evens out and I feel a sense of peace when the cool air touches my skin and slips into my lungs.

I might hate it, but it's the closest thing to a real home I've ever known. Memories of going to games with my dad, him taking me to practice or to just goof around together… I shake those memories back and focus on the present.

Moo U hockey is a big deal. Not only to hockey fans, but to the entire student body. Weekends are for hockey or frat parties. You can go to one or both, but if you go to neither, people look at you confused like what else could you possibly be doing?

Once the game starts, I don't have any more time to second-guess the job or bemoan my hatred for hockey. At first, I'm too caught up in the job, dreading the moment someone needs me to do something—refilling water bottles after each use, trying to appear busy.

Eventually the action begs for my attention. The team is young, and they make mistakes you'd expect college players to make, but they're dominating the puck.

Patrick Graham makes a goal off a rebound by Weston Griggs seconds before the end of the first period. The guys on the ice celebrate and then they all head off to the locker room with huge grins on their faces.

One down, two more to go. Times about thirty more games. Ugh.

I have just enough free time between periods to clean up the bench, check on Northeastern, and jog back to the Moo U bench before intermission ends. I should have eaten or grabbed a coffee before the game. Oh wait, I'm broke. Well, not totally broke, thanks to Vivian.

Coach Garfunkle and Coach Keller are talking with one of the players as I take my spot behind the bench. Number twenty-three, Lex Vonne, left-handed forward, size eleven skates, uses a ninety-flex stick. Oh, god, that file Alec put together was too good. I've memorized the entire roster and that is not something I'm proud of. At all.

Lex skates back and forth a few times while the coaches watch him. He's a good-looking guy if you're into that blond hair, brown-eyed, cleft chin, perfect body kind of hockey dude. A frown pulls at his pouty lips. "It doesn't feel right. Something's different."

Coach Garfunkle stares at his skates as he continues to glide. "We can re-sharpen them after the game or swap you out for another pair of skates now?"

Before I realize I'm being helpful, I stand and move closer. "I'll grab another size eleven from the locker room."

"Nah." Lex shakes his head and steps up to the bench. He played less than two minutes of the last period, but he's got that same determined and focused look the others wear. "They'll be okay for tonight."

"You're sure?" Coach Garfunkle asks.

Lex glances to me and then quickly looks away. "They're fine."

I feel some ridiculous resentment that he won't let me do my job, but I can't tell if it's because he doesn't trust me not to screw it up or because he's one of those guys who thinks if he switches skates halfway through a game he'll give the team bad juju. Hockey players are ridiculously superstitious.

Both coaches briefly look to me for help as if they expect me to convince this kid to switch skates. I shrug. "He says it's fine."

And fine is great because it means less work for me.

LEX

The guys are celebrating our win tonight as I head to see our new equipment manager. For once, I can blame my shitty game on someone else. Whatever she did to my skates, I felt like Bambi standing for the first time out there.

"Hey, uh, can you sharpen these for tomorrow?" I ask, holding out my skates. "Half-inch radius."

She stares blankly, blinking a few times. "Your file says five-eighths."

Okay, so maybe not completely her fault. "Alec had me try it, but I like the half-inch."

"Okay." She takes my skates. I'm sort of impressed that she doesn't cringe or make a big deal out of the smell because it's not roses.

"Could you replace the lace on the left one, too? It's frayed."

"How old are these skates?"

I shrug and then straighten my shoulders. "Not that old."

Three years and I think they were used when I got them, but I like my skates. I get plenty of shit from the guys about them. Most of the team has newer ones from Dalager, but I prefer mine.

Kaitlyn looks like she wants to say more about my beat-up skates but doesn't. "Okay. I'll re-sharpen them and replace the laces before Monday."

"Can you do it tonight?"

"You guys are off tomorrow."

"No official practice, but I usually come in."

I don't move and neither does she. I try to see Declan Dalager in her, but aside from the blue eyes, she looks nothing like him. Her hair is a shiny brown, and she has high cheekbones that seem vicious when she purses her full lips, like she's doing right now.

"Please?" I don't think I ever had to say please with Alec. He was always willing to do anything we asked. Kaitlyn is not Alec.

She's beautiful. Average height, but she's thin and the heeled boots she's wearing make her seem even taller. Still, she has a fragile quality about her like a pristine china doll.

"Fine. I'll do it tonight. Is there anything else?"

She's intimidating, so at least she has that in common with her dad. I looked him up last night. Yeah, I'd heard of him but hadn't really bothered to check him out. The guy really was a legend. I spent three hours watching old clips in my room. I'm sure the guys would have loved to watch with me, but then again, they've probably already seen them.

I often feel like the outcast when it comes to that stuff. I didn't follow hockey as a kid, so I didn't have heroes like Declan Dalager or Tony Amonte.

Shit, I'm still staring. "No, uh, I don't think so."

"Great." She gives me her back, turning on those heels. Her ponytail waves behind her.

I walk over to the Biscuit with Paxton and Ash. Patrick,

Tate, Weston and Jonah are at our usual table and already have beers in front of them. I'm not in a great headspace. Two games where I sat on the bench so much I think there might be an imprint of my ass. I already work harder than the rest of the guys. Early morning runs, no off days. Still, I'm not where I need to be and I'm running out of patience and opportunities.

Our server arrives before we've taken our seats. We're very good customers, so they take excellent care of us. This girl in particular, Gail, seems to have a serious crush on my teammate Weston. She stands near him at the other end of the table and we bark out our orders. Politely bark of course.

"Where's Maggie tonight?" Patrick teases Tate. "Your lap looks lonely."

Tate grins. He does that a lot these days. "She was at the game, but she went with her family to dinner. They might stop by later."

"How sweet," Patrick says like it's anything but. Then he glances around our local hangout. "I'm gonna walk around, see who's here."

We all do our own perusal. There's a lot of girls here tonight. A lot of people, period. Patrick and Jonah stand and weave through people to get to the cute girls sitting at the bar.

"Did you get your skates worked out?" Paxton asks while we wait for our wings.

"She's going to fix them tonight. Alec wrote down the wrong numbers. I was skating on five-eighths."

"Ah." He nods in understanding and takes another drink from his glass of beer.

We're silent, but the noise of the place provides a comfortable background noise.

"Do you really think her dad sent her to spy on us?" I ask. I can't get her off my mind. My high school's team manager and Alec were so different. They were excited and beyond helpful.

Real members of the team. Kaitlyn didn't seem happy to be there at all.

"Who?" Ash asks.

"Kaitlyn." I glance around. She isn't here. Alec always came out with us to celebrate, but something tells me we won't be seeing her.

"For what purpose?" Pax asks.

"I don't know." I shake my head. "She did not look happy to be working for us though. I wonder why Coach hired her."

"Dude, stop talking about hockey and look around," Kirk, our goalie and most annoying member of the team, says. "All of these people came to celebrate with us and to hook up with us. These girls don't care if you played a second of tonight's game. You're a hockey player. Enjoy." He waves his hands out in front of him in a big, theatrical display.

"He's an idiot, but also not wrong. You can't fix anything tonight." Paxton cocks his head to one side.

"Wise words, my man," Ash says, and then turns to make room for Patrick and Jonah and the three girls they brought back to the table.

"We'll work on it Sunday." Paxton nudges me.

"Thank you."

More girls drift over to our table. It's like breaking the seal. Once one girl joins, all the others flock to join. And we make room for them. We're a welcoming group—some more than others. Kirk is a great goalie, and the chicks dig him for reasons I'll never comprehend. His girl of the night is creeping on my space.

I politely nudge her. "Can you move over a little? Your hair is in my beer."

Kirk glances around her. "Sweetie, you got any friends that could show Rook here a good time for his efforts tonight? He's having a little bit of a dry spell on and off the ice, if you know what I mean." He winks at me like he's doing me some big favor.

I suppress a groan. Yeah, just what I want—a chick sleeping with me out of pity or because I play hockey. That's not to say I don't enjoy the attention that comes with being a part of Moo U's hockey team, but every time a girl approaches me with the team it's clear she wants to hook up with my jersey and not me. Being interchangeable isn't something I'm into.

We don't need to share our life history but knowing my name—so I can make her scream it—is necessary.

"Yo, yo," Ash says in a hushed tone looking toward the door. We all follow his gaze to the doorway where Kaitlyn stands with another girl I've never seen before. Every head in the place turns to look at them.

They're both stunning, but my attention is quickly drawn back to Kaitlyn. She looks uncomfortable for a moment as she glances around the bar. When she spots our table, her shoulders straighten.

She's changed clothes from the black pants and green polo uniform to a short dress. Her hair is down. The light-brown locks fall past her shoulders.

The two girls head toward a table across the restaurant. Still, I keep watching. Kaitlyn unwraps a long, green scarf from around her neck and shrugs out of her coat.

I stopped listening to the guys at some point, but Ash gets my attention as he pushes back on his barstool. "I'm going over to talk to her, invite her to sit with us."

Pax puts a hand on his shoulder. "If she wanted to talk to us, I think she would have done that sometime during the past three hours she was around us."

"Did the ice queen talk to anyone?" Patrick asks.

Everyone's quiet for a beat.

"I walked by the equipment room to see if she could

repair my pad, but she shot me a death glare and I decided I didn't really need it fixed," someone says. That earns some laughs.

"I talked to her," I say finally.

They all look to me.

"I asked her to re-sharpen my skates tonight so I could practice tomorrow."

A deep groan that I'm pretty sure comes from Patrick—it's his primary mode of conversation when talking to me—is followed by Ash's great idea. "You should go over and talk to her then, Vonne."

"No." I quickly dismiss the idea. "What would I even say?"

"Come on," Jonah pushes. "Someone should at least go say hello now that we're all staring at her. It's going to be a long season if our manager isn't doing her job."

Patrick wipes his mouth with the back of his hand. "I normally wouldn't recommend breaking the ice with a girl by chatting hockey, but this might be the one instance in which your obsession with talking hockey at the bar comes in handy. Reel her in, Vonne."

"She's not a fish."

"Nah, but she's fucking cold-blooded from what I hear, and we need her on our side."

She didn't really come off that way to me. I don't mind hard, difficult things though. Might even say I prefer them.

Kirk laughs. "He couldn't get a girl like Kaitlyn Dalager. She's way out of his league."

Frustration burns. Asshole dares don't normally push me into action, but I'm tired of being underestimated. I can play with these guys and I can damn well get a girl like Kaitlyn if I wanted.

Pushing back from the table, I stand and take my beer with me. Something to do with my hands. I can hear the guys chuckling behind me. Patrick yells for me to give her a wide berth.

Aware they are watching my every move, I slow my pace and consider what I'm going to say. Unfortunately, I don't come up with anything before I get there.

Her friend spots me first. I smile and her red lips fall into a frown. Awesome, another fan.

I consider doing a drive-by and circling back to the boys. Pretend I'm lost or going to talk to someone else, anyone else. That'd probably be a smarter choice, but I'm feeling just dumb enough that instead I jut my chin in greeting and stop at the end of their table. "Hey there."

It's crickets. Her friend gives me a look that makes my balls want to climb inside my body and hide. I turn my focus on Kaitlyn and offer her a big smile that she does not return.

"Hi?" She says it slowly like it's a question and looks around. "Are you lost?"

"I don't think so." I sit beside her. She's in the middle of the booth, so I'm closer than would be considered casual. Something floral hits my nose and our arms brush. She doesn't scoot over to make room for me, and I sort of dig the way she holds her ground. Most people would move over to be polite, even if I'm the one being rude by sitting. Not Kaitlyn.

"Yes, please, sit down." Her words drip with sarcasm.

"Thanks."

"Read the table," her friend says.

I angle so I can't see the death stare that her hater friend's giving me. Kaitlyn looks more amused than pissed.

"Listen," I say. "I wanted to say sorry about the whole mix-up with my skates."

The waitress drops off their drinks and smiles at me. "Can I get you something?"

"He's not with us," Kaitlyn says.

"I'll have another beer. Thanks."

"Look…" Kaitlyn starts and then pretends like she doesn't know my name. The way she had my skate size and blade radius memorized, I refuse to believe she doesn't know the whole roster.

"Lex." I hold out my hand.

Her blue eyes drop to it, but she doesn't slide hers into mine. Instead, she peers around me, scoffs, and then rolls her eyes. "Go back to your teammates. Whatever they dared you to do—I'm not interested."

The waitress reappears and sets my beer down in front of me. "Here you go," she says cheerily.

I thank her and then refocus my attention on Kaitlyn. "I can't do that until I've properly welcomed you to the team. We're excited to get to know you. Plus, I like it better over here. You smell nicer."

"I smell nicer than a bunch of hockey players. What a compliment."

"Truth," I say. "Kirk didn't shower after the game. He says the ladies like the fresh stench on him after a game."

Kaitlyn makes a face.

"Right?" Finally, a little common ground. Not showering after playing hockey is gross. I'll take what I can get. "So, I heard you transferred here this year. Where from?"

She doesn't respond.

"Come on. Tell me something. I'm trying to get to know you. I think you're kind of fascinating." And I really do for reasons I don't even understand.

"I'll bet," she says dryly. "Me or my dad?"

"Both, I guess." I shrug. "I didn't know much about him until I got to Moo U, but the guys said he—"

"No, we're not doing this."

"Why not? Are you not interesting enough to hold a conversation?" I tease her.

She scoffs. "Like you would notice either way."

"I'm sorry, did I not just walk over here to talk to you?" I chuckle at her clear refusal of my every attempt to get to know her. I've never met anyone like her, that's for sure.

She invades my space, runs a finger up my arm and then twists the hair at the nape of my neck. Chills shoot down the left side of my body. Her body is arched toward mine at an angle that pushes out her tits. I try not to notice, but well… I fail. She's got a nice rack. And judging by the low-cut of her dress that reveals part of her bra, I think people noticing was kind of the point.

"What do you want to know?" she asks. "What the great Declan Dalager is up to? See if I can maybe get you some face time or an autograph?"

I'm completely frozen and apparently unable to speak. She moves even closer so that her tits are now pressed against my chest and her blue eyes bore into me through thick black lashes. "Or maybe you were hoping we could just get out of here. Maybe a quick fuck in the parking lot to help celebrate the win? Is your car outside?"

My gaze drops to her parted lips. "I, uh…"

"Go back to your own crowd, Lex Vonne. I don't sleep with hockey players and you're not going to use me to get to my father."

I knew she knew my name!

The space between us now that she's moved away feels cold and I desperately want to close it. Who the hell is this chick?

"Hockey *bro*," her friend says. "We're not interested."

"What's wrong with hockey players?"

"We don't have enough time before last call for me to answer that." Her friend takes a sip of her drink.

"I don't get it," I say to Kaitlyn. Forgetting that her dad is a hockey player completely, why would she take a job working with hockey players if she disliked us so much?

"Let me help clear things up." Again the friend interrupts, though this time it's with my beer in her hand. She chucks the contents in my face. Her smug smile is the last thing I see before beer stings my eyes and drenches my shirt.

"Oh my god, Viv," Kaitlyn says through a look of horror that's quickly followed by laughter.

"Thanks for that." I wring out my shirt onto the floor. The waitress is already at my side with napkins which I accept. "Really good talking to you. It was definitely interesting."

I stomp back to my boys. Their cackling laughter reaches all the way across the room.

Patrick slaps a hand on my shoulder and a fresh burst a laughter explodes from the table as beer sloshes off my shirt.

"How'd it go?" he asks, biting back his own laughter.

I take a seat. "Well, I'm not thinking about hockey anymore."

KAITLYN

"You got some of that on me," I whine to Vivian. We moved tables, but there's still a wet spot on my dress from the beer my best friend tossed in Lex's face.

A tad dramatic? Yes.

Absolutely hilarious? Also, yes.

I do feel a little bad for the guy, but not enough to apologize.

"Do you think he's going to sit over there all night in wet clothes?" She smirks, obviously pleased with herself.

"I don't know, and I don't care." I steal a quick glance in his direction. His white T-shirt clings to his body and a cute redhead is attempting to pat him dry with a napkin. He doesn't seem all that fazed by the beer-soaked shirt or the redhead.

"He's kind of hot."

I grunt an acknowledgment. "Should we get another round and then go to the multicultural house?"

"I think tonight is a night for shots. And I'm not ready to leave yet. The eye candy is too good in here."

"They're all hockey players."

"Shh. You're ruining it."

The Biscuit is the hockey guys' hang out and not somewhere I'd usually come, but Vivian insisted we stop by so she could prove that she was behind me and my new job. Her hatred for hockey players runs deep, but her support of me is unwavering. At least in the two months since we've become friends.

"Why do you hate hockey players anyway?" I ask. She's never said, and I never thought to ask until now.

"Why do you?" she asks with a mocking glint that says she knows I'm not about to open up. I guess there's a reason we haven't discussed it before. Vivian and I's friendship is built on a foundation of ambiguous backstories and a shared disdain for lots of things. We don't ask the other to provide anything we don't want to tell. Not because we don't care, but because neither of us is big on sharing.

"I don't hate hockey players. I hate hockey."

"Same difference."

Fair enough.

Our waitress approaches. She's not nearly as smiley now that Lex is gone. "Are you two doing okay?"

"Another round," Vivian tells her. When I groan, she says, "Admit it, you're not ready to leave either."

"I can't let them run me off." I need to show them I can hold my own.

"Oh, looks like he's leaving. Guess he isn't going to sit there with a wet crotch all night. Too bad. He was fun to look at."

I snort-laugh and turn slightly to see Lex walking toward the door. He's staring at me with a cocky tilt of his lips. As soon as our eyes meet, I turn back around.

"Good riddance."

Our waitress returns with our drinks and two shots.

"We didn't order those," Vivian says as the server sets each one on the table.

"The guy that was sitting with you earlier ordered them. He said to let you know there's a party at the hockey house tonight."

Vivian's eyes light up. She's a funny one. The second a hockey player hits on her, she scares them off, but now she wants to follow them around to look at them. They're not *THAT* hot. Most of them anyway.

"We're not going."

"Boo, you're no fun." She holds up a shot glass. "To your new job."

The next afternoon, I head over to the rink to organize the equipment closet and finish the laundry from last night. I'm nursing a headache and my stomach is queasy. I haven't been this hungover in a long time.

The more Vivian drank, the more I learned about her hatred for hockey players. More specifically THE ONE who broke her adolescent heart. The more she told me, the more shots she ordered, and well, I couldn't make her drink them alone.

The locker room and adjoining offices are empty. Once the first load of laundry is going, I take a seat on the edge of the small desk in the equipment manager's closet to look through the tablet and see if I can figure out the organization system Alec was using. My phone vibrates in my pocket. I expect it to be Vivian calling to hang out. Lately, our typical Sunday has consisted of grabbing coffee and then hanging out at her apartment. It gives me a short reprieve from the dorms and Vivian and I watch TV, gossip, paint our nails… all the usual girl stuff that gets pushed during the week while we have classes.

Instead of Vivian, though, it's my dad. I stare at his name on the screen until it goes to voicemail. Then, I bring up our last text exchange.

The man is an NHL Hall of Famer and runs a multi-million-dollar company, but his texts are a rambling of run-on sentences and misspellings as if he couldn't be bothered to use his precious time to double-check them before sending. *Checking in. How's VT? Classes goin okay? Be looking forward to seeing your grades at semester. See you at thankssgvng.*

That was a month ago and I replied with the standard, *I'm fine. Everything's fine.* I left off the eye roll emoji, but I definitely rolled my eyes while I tapped out the message.

I haven't told him about my job, so I send a quick, *Can't talk now. I'll call later.*

I keep staring, waiting for a follow-up or some acknowledgment that doesn't come. Figures. Everything is on his schedule. He probably crossed me off his to-do list as soon as he hit voicemail and then moved on to his next task. He does call every week and attempt to check in—I'll give him that. Though he also sent me to freaking Vermont so I'm a little salty.

Voices carry from the locker room, but I can't make them out. Last night was a real wake-up call. I'm going to have to interact with these guys. They're going to expect it. So is Coach Keller. I'm here to wait on them. Ugh.

Shoving my phone in my pocket, I get back to work.

I allow myself to admire the Dalager equipment. When I was little, I knew each design, the model number, how much it sold for, and had talking pieces for each one. My dad said I was a born marketer, but back then I was just so proud of what he'd created I memorized every fact sheet for talking points to sound like I knew what I was talking about.

Since then, the company has evolved and grown. It's still impressive, though. I pick up a stick and hold it out. It's too heavy for me, but I still admire its strength and elegance. Goose bumps dot my arm as I place it back on the wall. Alec has them organized in numerical order for the players—or well, he did.

I recapture his organization of the sticks and then move on to skates and helmets, then pads. My stomach growls and I've lost all track of time when I'm finally pleased with the small equipment room.

"Hey, Kaitlyn," Coach Keller scares the bejesus out of me as he says my name in the doorway.

"Hey." I place a hand over my heart. "Sorry, I guess I was in deep concentration."

"The place looks great."

"Thank you." It really does. I'm sort of surprised with myself.

"If you get a chance, can you take the water cooler out to the bench."

"Oh, sure. Is that something Alec did?"

"Yeah. We don't officially have practices on Sundays but some of the guys like to come in."

"Sure, I'm just finishing up in here. I'll take it out now. Anything else?"

"Nah, enjoy your Sunday."

I lug the large cooler out to the bench.

Lex, Ash, and the Graham twins are on the ice. Paxton is standing off to the side watching while the other three skate hard from one end toward the other. Patrick handles the puck as he skates down the ice. He sends a short pass to Ash on his right. Ash sends it sailing to the left side where Lex drops it into the empty net.

I stumble and nearly drop the cooler. The noise gets Paxton's attention. He rushes to help me, and we maneuver it in place.

"Thanks. We could have helped you with that."

"You just did."

"Well, I mean next time. Before you try to carry it out here yourself, ask. That's what freshmen are for." Paxton Graham, one of Moo U's star players regards me with a sincere smile. There are too many nice guys on this team making it hard to hate them.

"Thanks, but I can handle it," I assure him. I will not appear weak in front of these guys. There's nothing worse than people thinking you've been given something because of your father. Even if that's exactly what happened here.

A gush of cool air halts me in my tracks as Lex skates up. He tears off his helmet and runs a hand through his blond hair. "How was that?" He asks Paxton. His gaze falls on me and I get a slight chin jut of acknowledgment before he looks back to Pax. "Can we do some more? Maybe three-man weave again?"

Paxton chuckles softly. "Take a breather, man."

Lex drops his helmet back on his head. "I'll work on face-offs with the guys while you slack off." He briefly glances at me again. "Hey, Kaitlyn. Have fun last night?"

"Certain parts were entertaining."

He smiles and then skates off.

"He's intense," I say when he's out of earshot.

"Lex is cool. He's got tunnel vision right now, trying to get more ice time during games. He's fast, left-handed, good stick skills…"

"What's the problem?" I'm sorry I asked almost instantly. *Do not get involved. You don't care.*

He leans on his stick. "He wants it too much. Too inside his own head. Focused on himself and not able to read the ice. He can't find a good rhythm with the rest of the guys and ultimately that means a lot more to the team."

"Well, good luck."

"Hey, wait. Maybe you can help."

"Me?"

"Yeah, Declan Dalager's daughter. He was legendary for seeing the ice. What would he say or do?" Admiration burns in his eyes.

"Oh, I don't know. I'm sure whatever Coach says is far more appropriate."

"Come on, yes you do. What would your dad say?"

I nod because I do know. Work harder than everyone else is practically the Dalager family motto. It's the way my dad approaches everything in life. Undeterred, unwavering dedication. It's admirable so long as you aren't the thing being tossed aside for someone's passion.

My gaze flits to Lex gliding across the ice, a look of determination and intense focus. It's commendable, but it's not enough. "He'd say there's only so much of your own time you should waste helping a person before you cut them loose."

Another family motto, the most important one, always prioritize what's best for yourself first.

LEX

"Hey. Going for a run?" Tate asks Monday morning when I stumble into the kitchen before dawn. He and Maggie are standing hip to hip next to the sink, drinking coffee out of matching green mugs.

"Yeah. What are you guys doing?"

"Gotta go out to the farm this morning." Tate's a local. So is his girlfriend Maggie. They have neighboring family farms just outside of town.

"Will you be back before weightlifting?" I ask, rubbing the sleep from my eyes.

"Probably be back before you're done with your run. How far are you going today?" He asks me and then looks to Maggie. "He ran six miles yesterday on our off day and then went to the rink to get in an extra practice."

"I'm not going that far today." I grab a glass of water and chug it to help me wake up. "Today I'm doing sprints."

"Don't push yourself too hard, rookie," Tate calls after me as I go out the back door of the house.

I walk around to the front and stretch. Getting up early isn't my favorite, but with classes all day, then practice, plus the extra sessions I get in with Paxton, this is the only time I have to work on speed training.

My speed is my biggest asset and I work my ass off to maintain it.

I start with some light step-ups using the steps off the front porch. The hockey house, where I live with some of my teammates, is an old Victorian. The wood floors creak, the windows are drafty, and it's nearly always noisy. Even guys on the team that live elsewhere spend a lot of time here. I love being in the middle of the chaos. And my small room is way cheaper than what I'd be forking over to live in the dorms.

Once my muscles are warm and the cool air has shocked my system awake, I sprint down the middle of the road. It's too early to worry about traffic, but I'm running faster than any car would be anyway.

I do a lot of variations. Sitting to sprint, split lunge to sprint. Hell, I even do some backward. My thighs are on fire and my throat burns from sucking in the cold air.

There's something about pushing myself at this level that rids all negative thoughts. I've always been good at focusing one-hundred-percent at a single thing. I get shit from the guys for pushing so hard, but hockey is why I'm here. Vermont, Burlington University specifically, is my opportunity to make hockey more than a hobby.

I'm going to get a degree while I'm here but I already know that doing anything but hockey after graduation will feel like I've failed.

When I get to the dining hall for breakfast, the guys are already seated at our usual table.

I drop down next to Jonah. He has his phone out and tilts it where I can see. "Watch this! Watch this!"

It's an old hockey clip. Burlington against Notre Dame. Shoveling in a bite of eggs, I ask, "What year is this?"

"Ninety-nine, I think. That's Dalager when he played for Burlington."

I watch as he takes the puck down the ice, dekes out a defender, and then makes a pass that surprises everyone. Even the guy it's intended for. The guy fumbles it but he's so wide open that extra second delay doesn't matter. The goalie is still watching the wrong side of the ice and Moo U scores.

Jonah shakes his head. "He was incredible. Always knew where his teammates were and found a way to get them the puck."

"Like Pax and Patrick," I say, still watching the screen. Those two have this freaky ability to read each other's thoughts. Some sort of twin psychic powers that make them damn hard to defend.

He sets his phone down. "Are you going to be dragging ass for practice today? Heard you were running sprints this morning."

"I'll be fine," I assure him. But I eat my weight in protein and healthy carbs just in case.

Kirk and Ash join us as I'm pushing back my plate.

"Rookie," Kirk says with a grin. "Get any more beer poured on you?"

With a chuckle, I shake my head. "Nah."

Our fiery equipment manager didn't give me so much as a second glance yesterday when I saw her at the rink. And, while I gave her third, fourth, and fifth glances, I didn't go out of my way to talk to her again. I have to keep my focus on hockey and get off that fourth line. I'd also like to avoid beer baths. I'm never living that down.

My phone buzzes in my pocket. "I gotta go. See you guys at practice."

"Hey," I answer after I drop off my tray.

"Lex!" My dad's boisterous voice makes me smile.

"What's up, old man?"

"Just checking in." I can hear the noise of the tire shop in the background. "Barely heard from you since school started."

"Sorry. I've been busy."

"Congrats on the game last weekend."

"You watched?" My dad is not exactly a hockey fan.

"Your brother did. He gave me the highlights. I was working late." No surprise there. I get my work ethic from my dad.

"Well, the team played well. We got another win. I had an issue with my skates and didn't play much." The white lie feels like acid on my lips. My family doesn't care if I play every second or none, but it's for precisely that reason that I want them to see me succeed.

Someone calls for my dad and he speaks away from the phone barking orders. "Sorry about that," he says to me. "Your brother is on a test drive and our new guy was a no-show."

"It's okay. I'm glad you called. How's everything there?"

"Busy, as always. Oh, before I forget, I deposited a little money into your bank account. It's not much, but maybe you can buy a decent coat. I saw on the weather channel there was a chance of snow there this weekend."

"I'll be fine. The cold doesn't bother me."

"Vermont cold is different. I did a run out there once when I was driving trucks. Broke down on the side of the road. Bitter cold."

"I'll wear a sweatshirt or borrow one of Tate's many flannels."

His laughter fills my ear. "When you get home next spring, it's going to take you all summer to thaw out."

With it being so far away and hockey running through the holiday breaks, I won't be able to go home again until the end of freshman year. Weird to think how long I'll go without seeing him.

He speaks away from the phone again telling someone he'll be right there.

"These yahoos can't manage five minutes without me," he grumbles. I think he secretly likes being indispensable. "I have to go. I'll call next week."

When I get to practice, the guys are smiling and laughing, gathered around together.

"It smells like flowers or… a tropical island." Jonah holds the collar of his jersey up to his nose and inhales.

"I don't like it." Patrick says. "It smells girly. I'm going to be distracted all practice."

"What's going on?" I ask, perplexed as the guys are all sniffing their jerseys.

"Check out your jersey. They're clean. Like smelly clean," Tate instructs.

I grab my jersey hanging in my stall and bring it up to my nose and then cough. "Are you fucking with me? This is awful. Did she even wash them?"

When I drop my jersey away from my face, I actually can smell a lingering floral scent—but it's definitely not coming from my jersey. Patrick steps closer and I can really smell it. It smells divine. Like laundry heaven.

I lean in to sniff him. "Clean smells girly?"

"Girls smell nice." He shrugs one shoulder and then lets out a low whistle. "Wow, that is ripe, Vonne."

He tosses it into his brother's face and soon my jersey is making the rounds to each guy for a whiff.

"So, mine is the only one that doesn't smell nice?" Since

Alec left our jerseys were usually washed but we've definitely gone a day or two in between. And sometimes when one of the other freshmen were in charge, they smelled faintly of mildew because they forgot to move them from the washer to the dryer.

Right now, mine smells like it was at the bottom of a week's worth of sweaty laundry.

Jonah cackles and the guys join in. "Oh man, you pissed off the equipment manager. Not smart."

"Did you check your gear?" Patrick asks.

"No, why?" My skates are waiting for me along with the rest of my gear. It looks okay as far as I can tell.

"Girls are crazy." He walks off with a wary look on his face. "Be careful, rookie."

I wait for the guys to head out to the ice and walk over to Kaitlyn. Her hair is pulled up on top of her head and she's got in her earbuds, probably to block us out.

I tap her on the shoulder and then step back to give her room.

She removes one ear bud.

"Hey!" Her tone is a warning. It's entirely too sweet. And she's smiling at me. Not in a good way—in a, *I may have just sabotaged your gear* way.

"I, uh, don't think my jersey got washed with the rest of the team's." I hold it up.

"That's odd." She narrows her gaze. "Are you sure you put it in the basket with the rest of the team's after last practice?"

"I'm sure." Ninety percent. Maybe seventy-five. I think she's fucking with me, but dammit her face gives nothing away.

"I have study group in fifteen, so it'll have to wait until tonight." Her smile stays intact.

"What am I supposed to wear for practice?"

"Everything else is in the laundry." She bats her lashes innocently. Okay, definitely fucking with me. "Sorry, stinky."

I'm sure this jersey has smelled worse, but I've never been more aware of it as I trudge out to the ice. The rest of my gear was intact. Or at least it seems that way so far. I swear the scent of lavender and soap hangs in the air, taunting me as we warm up.

The guys give me crap throughout practice. And a wide berth. The people that weren't at the Biscuit the other night get filled in. Though the events seem to get twisted and escalated each time it's retold.

Even Coach bites back a laugh at my expense when Patrick informs him that I hit on the equipment manager and she's exacting her revenge.

"So, what's the plan?" Tate asks when we're finished, and I can finally take off the offensive jersey that's made me the punchline of the day.

"Plan?"

"For getting back in Kaitlyn's good graces?"

"I didn't do anything. I was nice to the chick. I tried to make conversation and get to know her."

"Well, you did something." He pulls his jersey over his head and holds it up with a smile. "How does this thing still smell clean? I like her." His expression goes serious. "Fix it. I don't want her to accidentally mix up our jerseys or decide to take out her anger at you on the whole team."

When everyone else is gone, I take my jersey to the equipment closet. Draping the fabric over the back of the chair, I scan the desk for pen and paper. I jot out a note asking her to pretty please wash my jersey. But then I have a better idea.

KAITLYN

I don't think I've smiled this much since I got to Burlington. But the memory of Lex's face as he held up that horrid smelling jersey is enough to make me grin all afternoon. I'm even smiling as I return to the arena later that night. I need to do the laundry—maybe even his jersey—and repair a few things.

I admit that it was an extreme way to show him I wasn't someone he could hit on at the bar, give me a few compliments and get the Declan Dalager life story, but if I let him slide, the others will do the same. Still, it gave me more pleasure than I expected. He's fun to mess with.

I'm smiling down at my phone, texting Vivian to see what her plans are later, when I walk into the equipment room.

Movement catches my eye and my steps falter.

"What are you doing here?"

Lex's eyes widen and then a slow smile pulls his lips into a cheeky grin that is hard to hate. "Laundry… well, sort of."

I huff a laugh at the pile of folded jerseys he's working on. "First time?"

"Doing my own laundry because our equipment manager has it out for me? Yeah."

"I meant doing laundry. Period."

"Nah. Though I usually cram several weeks of dirty clothes into a single load and I'm afraid I'm hopeless at folding." He gives up pleating the jersey he's holding and drops it to the table.

I forget myself and laugh again. "Don't hurt yourself. I've got it."

"Just making sure my jersey made it in."

Silently, I move to the sewing machine.

"And hoping to get on your good side again. I'm sorry about the other night. The guys did send me over, but I really did want to get to know you."

Translation, he wanted to know more about growing up with the great Declan Dalager.

"Don't flatter yourself. I've not thought about any of you enough to divide you into columns of good or bad."

"No? Because I'm the only guy whose jersey missed the good smelling magic you worked in here."

"It's called laundry detergent. How long exactly did you guys go without someone doing your laundry? Never mind, I don't want to know."

"We took turns. Captain had us compete to decide who had to do laundry. I never lose a shootout."

"Of course you don't."

Lex leans against the table. "So, what's your deal?"

"I don't have a deal."

"What are you into? What do you do for fun?"

"I like long walks on the beach, pina coladas, and working in silence. Alone."

He shakes his head slowly. "All right. I can take a hint."

"Could have fooled me," I mutter under my breath.

He pushes off the desk and I can hear him moving behind me. "I put all the equipment back and wiped down the benches in the locker room."

I grunt a response that's not exactly appreciative but acknowledges his words.

"You're welcome," he singsongs, his voice getting farther away. "Later Kaitlyn."

I don't turn around or move until I've finished the repairs, but when I do it's to fully appreciate the clean locker room and organized equipment.

The team has a series of away games this weekend, so Friday afternoon I'm packing up all the equipment and trying not to think about spending two days surrounded by hockey players.

As I'm lugging the first bag out to the bus, the guys start to arrive.

"Hey." Lex falls into step beside me. "Let me get that."

"I've got it."

His hand closes around the strap next to mine. Warm, calloused fingers that shoot fireworks up my arm.

I pull away but he doesn't let go.

"What, because I'm a girl I can't possibly carry the heavy bags all by myself?"

"Can, but why would you?"

"Because it's my job."

He chuckles. "It's your job to make sure the equipment makes it on the bus. Not to carry it. That's what freshmen are for. Or that's what Alec did."

The first thing that Alec did that I agree with. I let go of the bag. "Fine, Freshman. There are three more, just as heavy, when you're done with that one."

He grins. The dimple in his chin is more pronounced when he smiles. "Got it."

"Yo, Forte, Roddy," he calls to two freshmen as he moves at a pace that is extra annoying since I know exactly how heavy that bag he's carrying is.

I watch to make sure the guys go back to get the other bags, but they do. Without comment. Huh. Maybe this job isn't so bad after all. Hockey players aside.

Once everything is loaded and all the players arrive, we're on our way. I sit up front across from Coach Garfunkle.

He lifts his word search. "Do you play?"

"No. Thanks."

He goes back to it and I stare out the window.

"Beef jerky?" a deep voice asks just as I'm about to drift off.

Lex moves my purse and sits beside me.

"I was saving that spot in hopes we picked up a cute hitch-hiker on the way."

"Hitchhikers are dangerous, Kait. Good thing I swooped in to save you." He holds out the bag of jerky.

I shake my head. "Yeah, good thing."

"Know any road games?"

"The silent game." I swear this guy brings out my sharp side. I think it's because in the past when guys were using me, I didn't see it coming. With Lex, it's so obvious. He's hardcore hockey with no apologies. I don't trust his friendly gestures.

"Never heard of it." He grins and rests an arm on the seat in front of us. He's a big guy. Two inches over six feet and just under two hundred pounds. Tall and muscular but not beefy. Still, his presence is a lot to take.

"Ever play slap hands?" He nudges me with an elbow, puts the jerky in the seat pocket, and then angles his body so he can hold out his hands, palms up.

"You're not serious?"

"Why not?"

"So many reasons."

"Come on. We've got two hours to kill."

"God, I must be desperate for entertainment," I mumble as I turn and place my hands on top of his.

Like before excitement and warmth jolts my nerve endings. My head knows he's playing me, but my body does not care.

"Ready?" he asks and brings his palms up so our hands touch from fingertips to wrist.

"Yes. No. Wait." I switch my hands so I'm on the bottom and in position to slap.

It takes three tries before I'm able to move my hands fast enough to smack his, but I'm ridiculously excited to have bested him. That is until it's his turn.

Again he brings his palms up, increasing the friction between our hands. I revel in the feeling too long and he strikes. I try to pull back but not fast enough.

"Oww." The sting of his slap turns the top of my hand red instantly.

"Oh shit, I'm sorry. I guess I'm used to playing with the guys." He takes my hand in his and rubs a thumb over the blotchy skin. "Are you okay?"

His brown eyes search mine and his brows draw together in concern. My heart is racing from the thrill of his touch and the look on his face. Like he cares if I'm okay. I've been fooled by that look too many times. Dylan was the last of many who made me feel special only to break my heart. And with Dylan it was even worse because he genuinely didn't care who my father was. Being dumped is awful, but being reminded that you're not worthy of love is gut wrenching.

I pull back and hold my hands to my chest. "I'm fine. That game is stupid."

It's chaos when we get to UMass. The freshmen once again carry the bags, but as soon as we're in the locker room I have to unpack and set up so we can get on the ice for warm-up.

I'm on the bench filling water bottles when they take the ice. Coach Garfunkle and Coach Keller are standing together watching.

"Forte is still favoring his right knee," Coach Garfunkle says. "Should we mix up the line? We've got Vonne."

Coach Keller crosses both arms over his chest, making his suit jacket bunch up around his armpits. "I'm not sure we have a choice. We need everyone healthy for next weekend. Dartmouth will be tough."

I find Lex on the ice and watch as he circles around the net. My gaze falls to his skates and I groan. Why the coaches have let him get away with wearing those old things is beyond me. It's one thing to be superstitious about your gear, it's another to wear skates that are way beyond being useful. He probably would like the five-eighths better if he had a stiffer boot. I'm surprised he hasn't seriously injured one or both of his ankles.

Thinking back to what Paxton said about Lex not finding a rhythm with the team, I watch him more carefully throughout the game. He doesn't play much so it's hard to tell how he meshes. What I can tell? He's frustrated. The hard set of his jaw and the way he skates—like his life depends on it.

Desperation. It's not any more effective scoring on the ice than off.

It's an ugly win, but a win none the less. The guys take the bus back to the hotel, but I stay behind to make sure everything is ready for tomorrow. We play UMass again tomorrow afternoon before we head back to Burlington.

When I finally make it to my room, I'm exhausted. Bone

tired. I need a shower and then I'm going to fall directly into bed. Turns out, this job isn't as easy as I thought. Especially now that the guys are getting more comfortable with me. I had a dozen requests after the game for repairs or adjustments.

I'm pulling on a T-shirt and leggings when there's a knock at my door.

I open it without looking, expecting one of the coaches doing rounds and checking rooms, but it's Lex on the other side. He's got a smirk and a bottle of wine.

"Are you lost?"

"Nope. A few of the guys are hanging out in the twins' room."

"How did you know this was my room?"

"Coach might have mentioned it when he was passing out room keys."

"Well, I'm tired and going to bed."

He places a hand on the door to keep me from shutting it. "Come on. Hang for a little while. We're not so bad."

"You have a game tomorrow."

"Yeah, but we're amped up from tonight's game. We need a few hours to wind down before we sleep." He laughs and drops his hand. "We're not doing coke off the coffee table and there're no hookers. Just a group of guys chilling. Come on."

I'm rooted in place as he takes a step down the hall. He looks back and seems surprised I haven't followed him.

I close my door and climb into bed. Lex Vonne is increasingly hard to dislike. I don't understand why he keeps pushing when I've made it clear that he's getting nothing from me. It's almost as if he really does want to get to know me.

LEX

Saturday's game is tough. It shouldn't be. UMass isn't all that good, but the twins are having an off day and that trickles down through the lines.

One plus is that I'm getting a little more ice time. Not that I'm doing much with the opportunity. I had another issue with my skates today and Kaitlyn had to swap the laces when I was off shift.

After the first period, we head to the locker room where we get a quick pep talk. I hang my head between my knees, giving myself a much more brutal kick in the ass than I'd ever get from the coaches.

"Vonne."

As I lift my head, Coach Garfunkle motions me over.

"What's up?" I ask, bracing myself for the worst. At this point, I'm probably lucky I'm stepping onto the ice at all.

"Kaitlyn wants to check your laces again before you head out."

She's in the small room adjoining the locker room where we have our extra equipment. Somehow she's made this small space look organized even with all the shit strewn around.

Bent over with her ass up in the air lining up skates, she's mumbling to herself, but I can't quite make out her words.

As much as I enjoy staring at Kaitlyn's butt, I've got a bench to park mine on.

"You wanted to see me?"

She snaps upright and turns so quickly her ponytail whips around her head and hits her in the face.

"Take off your skates," she instructs.

"The laces are fine."

"Great. Take off your skates." She picks up a pair of Dalager skates from the floor and holds them out. "Try these. They're about a decade newer than the ones on your feet."

"Thanks, but I'm good."

I start to walk off, but her annoyed sigh stops me. "Your boots are trash. These are stiffer and will give you more support, so you don't have to lace yourself in so tight you snap laces every other week. When we get back to Burlington, let's try the five-eighths radius again. Alec had the right idea, I think. You just needed to try them on a different skate." She shoves the skates against my chest and blazes past me out of the room.

"About time," Patrick says when he sees me carrying the new skates back to my stall.

"I don't think it's a good idea. I'm used to these." I look down at my old skates. They've been repaired a bunch of times and they look a little rough, but they're broken in and I like them. They've worked hard, like me. My dad bought them for me. He had no idea what he was buying, but it meant something to me that he'd put in the effort and spent the money.

We weren't scraping by exactly, but shelling out cash for things he deemed as a hobby or unnecessary wasn't my dad's way. And hockey fit both of those categories. It's something to pass the time while I get an education. He hasn't outright said it, but he's hinted enough that I know he's waiting for me to come to terms with my future working for him.

Selling tires, fixing tires—it's a fine way to make a living. But somewhere deep down I know that if that's where I end up, I'll feel like I failed. I'm meant to play hockey. I can't be this passionate and excited about something and it not be my purpose. I'll work as hard as I have to.

I put on the new skates and lace them up trying not to think too hard about it. I can try these during our warm-up before the second period and switch back when I don't like them. That'll appease Kaitlyn and she'll leave me alone about my skates. Hopefully.

She's in the tunnel watching as we walk back out. Arms crossed at her stomach, she looks each of us over as we pass by. The corners of her mouth pull higher when her gaze hits my skates.

When I step on the ice, I push off and go through my usual routine. The skates squeeze my feet something awful. I prefer a tighter fit—evidenced by the many laces I've sacrificed—but these aren't broken in so they're especially hard and uncomfortable. Totally impossible for me to play in.

Kaitlyn is helping Kirk with his pads when I head back to the locker room. I hurry so I can make it back in time before the start of the second. I left my old skates in my stall, but I don't see them. I'm looking all around in case I put them in someone else's spot, but it's like they grew legs and walked off on their own.

"Let me guess, you don't like the skates because they're too tight?" Kaitlyn's tone is annoyed. It matches her glare.

"Where are they?"

"Give the new skates a chance. You barely had them on five minutes."

"Five more and my feet will be numb."

"They won't."

I grit my teeth. "I want my skates back."

"And I want to be in New York sipping on an iced ginger coconut milk." She sighs. "Just try them for the second period. You're thinking about them now, but you won't be when you're in the middle of the game. That's where you'll give them a fair shot."

"And then you'll give me my lucky skates back?"

Her brows raise. "Lucky?"

"Do we have a deal?"

"Two shifts," she counters.

"Fine, but you owe me."

"For doing my job?"

I don't answer and she starts back to the bench. When we're almost out of the tunnel, she pauses to let me go ahead. "Equipment, gear, routine… it isn't lucky. They're tools. You hold your own luck." Her features soften. "My dad used to say that."

"I, uh…" Well, shit. I have no idea what to say. The buzzer sounds interrupting the moment and I don't have to worry about it.

Pat wins the face-off, and the second period is underway. I move my feet around in my skates while I wait on the bench. I don't have a great feeling about skating in them, but I don't ever want to have to put these back on, so I'll do my two shifts.

The first time I get out, my skates barely touch the ice before Tate gets called for high-sticking. He goes off to the box and Coach sends in our first line to stop UMass from capitalizing on the power play.

I get my next opportunity after Jonah scores off a wrister from Ash. The third line comes off the ice and Scoville, Thomas, and I go out.

We've got a little momentum and a lot of adrenaline. There's only thirty seconds left in the period. This is how it goes for the fourth line. Small opportunities that you have to take advantage of before you take a seat and watch the next ten minutes.

I'm only vaguely aware of the tightness of my skates and the way it feels when I make a quick turn to snatch a sloppy pass that goes high and gets away from UMass. Once the puck touches my stick, I could have snapping turtles on my feet and I probably wouldn't notice.

Avoiding two defenders, I send the puck to Scoville on the right side. He has it batted away, and they battle for it up against the boards before my teammate manages to slap it in front of the net. I beat their goalie to it and take it behind the net and around to the left side. Thomas is in position on the right side but a pass between the UMass defenders is too risky, so I take it toward the net myself. I aim for the five-hole and the goalpost lights up.

For three crazy seconds, I'm not sure if this is real life. Did I just score my first college goal? Thomas barrels into me. "Fuck, yeah. Nice work, Vonne."

The rest of the guys on the ice join him and then we skate by the bench where my entire team stands to congratulate me. I feel on top of the fucking world as they all bump my glove and tap me on the head. It's the first time I've felt like I contributed, and it feels fantastic.

And at the very end of the line is Kaitlyn with the biggest, smuggest smile I've ever seen.

The bus ride back to Burlington is filled with singing, a lot of loud chatting and laughter, and making plans for hitting up the Biscuit as soon as we get back. We've won every game this season, but this is the first time I've felt like I could really celebrate. I had a part in this.

I didn't do it alone though.

Kaitlyn is at the front of the bus in her same seat, but she made a point of putting her bag next to the window and sitting next to the aisle. I can't say for sure it was to keep me from sitting there again, but it seems likely.

I can't quite make out what her deal is. She knows a lot about hockey but doesn't seem to enjoy being around it. She's good at her job, but not enthusiastic about being part of the team. Maybe her dad did force her into the job. But why, I can't even imagine.

We make it back and everyone is eager to get going. The Biscuit will be nuts tonight. Any time we win, the place is crawling with people to help us celebrate.

"Daniels," I call to him and then the other freshmen when we're off the bus. "Grab a bag."

Kaitlyn's already got one large bag and Coach Garfunkle pulls the others out and sets them on the ground beside the bus.

"Question. Why did we hire an equipment manager if we were going to carry all the shit ourselves?" Jonah asks.

Cringing, I check to see if Kaitlyn heard. Yep. Totally outed. Her mouth opens, probably to yell at me, but I push Jonah forward and grab the biggest one myself.

"What the hell are you complaining about, man? We pack more extra sticks for you than any other guy."

He chuckles, and I let him and Hudson go ahead.

I fall into step with Kaitlyn and take her bag. Surprisingly, she lets me. "So, Alec didn't make the freshmen carry the equipment. He should have. What a bunch of whiny assholes we are."

She huffs a laugh. "I won't argue that."

I manage to get the door and hold it open while she steps through. Jonah and Hudson pass us on their way out.

"You need a ride, Vonne?" Jonah asks.

"I'll meet you guys there," I tell them and then follow Kaitlyn into the building.

She flips on the light in the equipment room and I drop the bags. "

"Are you coming out tonight? We're going to the Biscuit."

"I don't think so. I think I'll enjoy the next twelve hours of freedom."

"We're not that bad." I motion to the bags. "Can I help you unpack?"

"No, I'm going to leave it for tomorrow. I've got it from here." She pauses and then reluctantly adds, "Thank you."

"You can thank me by coming out tonight." I'd really like to spend more time with her to better understand why my pulse quickens when she's nearby. I don't think it's just because she's a challenge. Plenty of girls have tried to get me to chase them. Those girls were playing games, but I don't think Kaitlyn is playing at anything.

She hums a response that isn't agreeable.

"Come on. We won. And thanks to you, I got my first college goal."

"Oh no. I don't want any of the thanks."

"Why not?"

"Accepting your thanks assumes responsibility. It was the skates. Perhaps they're lucky."

"You don't believe that and neither do I. I think you're my lucky charm."

And I kind of do. I definitely want to spend more time with her to find out why I like being around her so much.

But something tells me pushing Kaitlyn will only make her

less likely to agree, so I glance around the room and ask again, "Are you sure you don't need any help?"

"I've got it."

I back out of the room. She looks up just before I disappear from sight.

"Congratulations, Lex."

KAITLYN

"No, I'm not going. This is stupid." I pace outside of the Biscuit, cursing my best friend. "You don't even like hockey players."

"No, but *everyone* will be at the Biscuit. The multicultural house is totally boring tonight. I'll catch a ride to you."

"I'm going back to the dorm." It took her two hours of texting me every few minutes to convince me to leave it and I've regretted it every step of the way.

"Absolutely not," Vivian's sharp tone screeches in my ear so loudly I pull the phone away. "Do not move. I'm getting in an Uber. I'll be there in five minutes. You left me all alone last night. Tonight, you're partying with me."

"Fine," I relent. "But when you get here, we're going somewhere else," I add, but she's already hung up.

I button up my coat and pace to keep warm. It started spitting snow as soon as I got here. Tiny flurries that make the dark of night look like a thousand pieces of paper have been shredded and dropped from the sky.

It's quiet outside, but every time someone opens the door, I can hear the loud noise of the busy bar inside. The hockey players will be at their usual table and everyone else will be crowded around to congratulate them and buy round after round.

It's so not my scene. Could it be? Sure. There've been moments hanging out with the team that I've enjoyed myself more than expected. Well, not the team. Moments with Lex. But of all the guys I could enjoy hanging out with, he's probably the one I should stay the farthest from.

He's everything I've tried to avoid since I was old enough that boys started using me to get closer to my dad. Eager, obsessed, hockey-focused. I know the type well. I was raised by one.

I sneak a glance behind me, but I don't let my eyes scan through the window long enough to recognize anyone. The door opens and I'm surprised when the guy I'm most nervous about seeing, stumbles out.

And he's definitely stumbling. Patrick steadies him while laughing. "All right, Vonne, easy."

"I'm fine. I'm fine," Lex says, pulling free like the stubborn guy he is and then swaying. Patrick backs him up against the building.

"I know. I know. You're perfectly capable all on your own," Pat says sarcastically. "Don't move." He stands in front of him and then his gaze flits to me. "Dalager."

I offer a small wave.

"Kaitlyn!" Lex yells and his eyes light up when he sees me. "You came!" He ambles over to me, creeping along the building. When he gets close, the smell of liquor hits me and I step back.

"Wowser. You got drunk fast."

"Shots. So many shots."

Patrick slaps him on the back. "Yeah, we each bought him a shot for his first goal."

"How many did he take?"

"Only about half of them," Pat says, like that isn't still way more alcohol than any one person should consume.

"It's okay because I'm really good at holding my liquor," Lex says through hooded eyes.

"Clearly." I take another step back.

Patrick chuckles. "Hey, Kait, are you waiting out here for a ride?"

"Uhh… Yeah." I nod. "I'm waiting for—"

"Awesome. Can you keep an eye on him? It's fucking cold out here." He doesn't wait for me to answer before speaking to Lex. "Pax is paying for his food, and then he'll be out to take you home. Congrats, buddy." He takes a step toward the door. "Thanks, Kaitlyn."

"You're welcome," I mumble as Patrick hustles back inside.

I sigh as Lex grins at me and leans in. "You look pretty."

"Oh, god." I have to pull my lips tight to stop from smiling. Drunk or not, his words warm my insides.

"What? You do. Would you rather I think you're ugly?"

"I'd rather you not notice me at all."

"I don't believe you." He invades my space even more. His fingers find the end of my scarf and he tugs lightly. "You came and you look pretty."

"I'm waiting for Vivian. I hadn't planned to go inside."

"Good thing I came outside then. How many different colors of these do you have?" He tugs the scarf again. This one is blue.

"A lot, I guess."

"I like to imagine which color you're going to wear every day."

This guy. He's too much.

"Let's go inside. Let me buy you a drink as a proper thank you for today." It's sort of cute he thinks he's in any condition to function well enough to walk, let alone buy me a drink.

"Consider it a gift to humanity. Those skates belonged in the trash."

"My dad bought those for me. First pair of new skates I ever owned. I bet you never had to worry about that."

"You're right. I was flush with hockey equipment."

"Sounds nice."

"Don't think for one second I had an easy life just because I grew up with money." My tone is harder than I intended.

"I don't think that. I don't really know anything about you. Not for lack of trying." The wind blows hard and I get a whiff of him. The alcohol and his body wash. "Tell me something about you." I open my mouth, and he holds up a finger and waggles it side to side. "And not some smart-ass comment. Something real."

"I..." My voice falters as his brown eyes are fixed on me. The way Lex looks at me makes me want to give him something, but my truths aren't on the table. "I'm going inside to wait for Vivian."

I take a step and then freeze. Dylan and Chastity are walking down the sidewalk hand in hand. Dylan sees me first. A slow smile tilts up one side of his mouth. While we didn't exactly say goodbye on the best terms, my ex is too nice to walk past me without stopping to say hello. He lifts his joined hand to get Chastity's attention and they lean close so he can whisper in her ear. I remember just what that used to feel like. Jealousy and sadness pour into my open wound. My roommate finally looks up to where I stand.

Quickly, I turn back to Lex. "Kiss me."

His brows pull together in confusion. And since I don't have the time to explain, I kiss him.

He has plenty of time to stop me. He doesn't. He steps even closer and brings a hand to my chin.

Full lips press back against mine. He isn't tender or reserved like I assumed. Greedy and consuming and everything I need to turn off the world for a few minutes.

His tongue seeks entrance and I give it to him. I open my mouth and lean into him so our bodies are flush. My body hums and sings for more while my brain shouts for me to flee. But Lex kisses like he plays hockey—desperate. And I think I've finally found the place that works for me.

The hand at my chin slides down and caresses my neck. His thumb rubs my skin tenderly as his lips press harder trying to get impossibly closer.

"Yo, Lex..." Pax's voice interrupts us, and I pull away quickly and bring a hand to my wet lips. I glance back to where Chastity and Dylan were, but they're gone.

"Woah, sorry. I didn't know you two—"

"I was just leaving," I say.

Pax holds up a hand. "None of my business. I'm going to get Tate's truck."

Lex waits until he's gone to ask the obvious. "Do I want to know what that was about, or should I just chalk it up to my drunk charm?"

"Definitely not the latter." My voice is shaky, but I'm not sure if it's from that kiss or seeing Dylan.

"Kaitlyn!" Vivian steps out of the back of her Uber. I put some distance between me and Lex. She might disown me if she knew I kissed him.

My insides are tangled, and I struggle to speak when she gets close. "Hey, you finally made it."

"I did, but it looks like I was too late to save you from bad company." Her gaze slides to Lex. "Hey, hockey boy. Want me to buy you a drink?"

Lex laughs.

"He was just leaving," I say as a beat-up truck pulls to the curb.

Pax rolls down the passenger side window. "Ready, Vonne?"

"Oh my god, I'm freezing. I left my coat at home. I'm going inside." Vivian rushes away.

"You want to come home with me?" Lex asks as he takes one step toward Pax's truck.

A surprised chuckle escapes my lips. "No." I take a step toward the bar. "And that's never happening again."

He smiles and continues to the curb where he opens the passenger door before calling back, "Night, Kaitlyn."

On Sunday, Vivian and I meet at The Green Bean to study. She's a sophomore art history major so we don't have any classes together but studying in my dorm is nearly impossible. Any time I'm there at the same time as Chastity, I'm hyper aware of every sound and movement next door. It's not just the sex that's hard to overhear. Every phone call or movie night. I can picture them so clearly because that was me.

I'm researching a class project for my digital marketing class while Vivian reads over her notes for a medieval art quiz.

"Do you know of any local businesses that I could use for my project?" I ask after I've spent fifteen minutes scrolling through local Burlington businesses and am ready to pull out my hair. Boring, boring, and boring. How many maple stores does one town really need?

"What's the criteria?"

"It's pretty open. Local, non-chain. But most of the popular downtown places have already been claimed. The Biscuit,

Tito's, The Green Bean..." I trail off listing the businesses my classmates swooped up while I was still snarling at the idea of writing a marketing plan for anything Vermont-related. "I'd like to use it for the internship interview, so it needs to be good."

My dream job is working at the premier marketing firm in Boston, Hawthorne Marketing. They have internships every summer for junior and senior college students. That's my in to secure a job for after graduation.

"What about Vino and Veritas?" Vivian suggests.

"The gay wine bar and bookstore?"

"Yeah. Have you been? It's such a genius idea for a business, and the place has a great vibe."

"I haven't, but it would be more interesting than trying to write a detailed marketing plan for some mom-and-pop café." And she's right, it's a genius idea which means the marketing should be a snap.

"I'll even come with you to research. They have this bartender, Rainn..." She looks to the ceiling with a dreamy, faraway look.

"Are all the bartenders gay?"

She shrugs. "No idea. He was hard to read, flirting with guys and girls."

"Well, I guess you can ask tomorrow. Are you free?"

"For this? Absolutely."

The following evening, I'm waiting for Vivian to pick me up outside of the arena. She's fifteen minutes late and not answering her phone.

Paxton and Lex walk out of the building. I've managed to avoid any one-on-one encounters with Lex since I kissed him

Saturday night, but it looks like my good fortune is about to run out. Curse Vivian. She's probably changing clothes for the tenth time, deciding what to wear while I pretend to look busy as Lex nods his head goodbye to Pax and heads toward me.

"Hey," he says when he's close.

"Hey," I say back in an uninviting tone.

"Looks like I was wrong today."

"About?"

"I guessed pink." His gaze briefly skirts over the black scarf wrapped around my neck. "Are you waiting for someone?"

My phone vibrates and I suppress a groan as I read Vivian's text, *Sorry, I totally forgot about a study session tonight. Make it up to you tomorrow!*

"Not anymore."

"Cool. Want to hang out?"

My gaze falls to his lips and I remember all too well what they felt like on mine. "No. I have somewhere I need to be."

"I thought you said you weren't waiting for anyone."

"Vivian and I were supposed to go somewhere together, but she had to bail."

"So, you're free?" He smirks.

"I still have somewhere to go."

He nods. "All right."

I hesitate for only a second before I decide that seeing Lex walk inside of a gay bar sounds more entertaining than going alone. "Do you want to come with me?"

"Absolutely. Besides, you owe me an explanation for the other night."

"I was hoping you were too drunk to remember."

"No chance."

We walk in silence down Main Street. The sun has set, and the wind whips my hair around my face. Lex is in jeans and a hoodie. His shoulders are shrugged up toward his ears and hands shoved in his pockets.

"Don't you own a coat?"

"Nah." He shakes his head. "Hardly ever needed one in Arizona. Even a sweatshirt was too warm most days in the winter."

At the corner, we stop to wait for traffic.

"Where are we going?" He removes his hands from his pockets and rubs them together. Long fingers, strong and veiny hands.

"It's just up on Church Street."

When the light turns and the crosswalk signals us, Lex takes my hand and pulls me along.

"Your hands are freezing," I complain. Somehow the cold seeping through his palm to mine radiates a warmth inside of me. As we approach our destination, I pull my hand free and motion to the building. "We're here."

KAITLYN

"I've heard of this place," Lex says as he holds open the door for me

"You have?"

Warmth greets me as I step inside. The bookstore is to the right. Beautiful shelves of hardcovers and paperbacks. I expected a small selection of books, but even without walking all the way in, I can tell it's a lot larger.

To the left is the bar area. I lead us past booths and tables to the bar.

I unbutton my coat and shrug it off as we take a seat.

"This place is cool," Lex continues to glance around the place taking it all in.

"You know this is a gay bar, right?"

"Yeah, some of the guys mentioned it." He doesn't look even the slightest bit uncomfortable. Even when a guy perched on a barstool beside him gives him a blatant once-over. "Vermont is the coolest."

"Hey, what can I get for you?" The bartender slides over to get our drink order. He's cute. Dark hair, striking blue eyes, and the kind of five o'clock shadow that makes you wonder what it'd feel like against your skin. This has to be the guy Vivian was talking about. Unless Vino and Veritas has another ridiculously hot bartender. In which case, this just became my new favorite bar.

"Can I try one of your hard ciders? Whichever one you recommend."

"Absolutely. I'll grab you my favorite." He glances to Lex.

"Same, I guess."

"IDs?"

I move for mine and Lex chuckles. "In that case, make mine a water."

"We've got a non-alcoholic cider if you want to try that?"

"Yeah, thanks, man. And can I see the food menu? Something smells amazing."

I place my ID on the bar top and he does a quick glance of it. Then grabs two menus and places them in front of us. "I'll be right back."

Lex wastes no time reading over the menu. He holds it up and reads aloud nearly every item like it's food porn.

"We have to try the maple pigs. Oooh, and a bacon cheeseburger sounds so good right now. Is that too much pig for one meal?" He looks to me thoughtfully and then shakes his head. "Maybe I'll just get a cheeseburger."

The bartender brings our drinks and Lex puts in a food order.

"You're not eating?" he asks when I hand my menu back.

I take a drink of my cider before responding. "No."

"Something against bar food?"

"No, I didn't come here to eat. It's research for a class project." Also, I'm still broke. I got my first paycheck and it's enough to cover food and true essentials, but I learned my lesson on cutting it too close.

"What kind of project?" Lex turns in his chair so that he's angled toward me.

"It's for my marketing design class. I have to do a report on a local business's online marketing. Website, advertising, social media—all of that. What are they doing well? What could they improve? It's worth a big chunk of my semester grade."

"Is that your major? Marketing?"

"Yes."

"I haven't decided yet."

"That's pretty common, I think. My friend, Vivian—"

"The one who threw beer on me," he interrupts.

"Yes, her. She's switched her major three times."

One side of his mouth pulls up into a smile and that dimple in his chin flirts with me. "Once I decide on something, I rarely change my mind."

My face warms as he continues to smirk at me. So much meaning in that statement.

I clear my throat. "This cider is really good. How's yours?"

He slides it to me. "Try it for yourself."

"Just describe it to me."

"It's cidery."

I laugh.

"Just try it. We've swapped spit. I think you're good to drink after me."

The bartender chuckles from behind the bar and I glare at Lex and then take a small sip of his cider, mostly to shut him up. But the non-alcoholic option is good too.

"Is this locally made?" I ask the bartender.

"Yeah. Made here in Vermont."

"Can I try a few more?" I ask. "Sample sizes."

"Sure. I'll grab a flight with our most popular alcoholic and non-alcoholic ciders."

"More research?" Lex asks.

"Yeah, and I just really want to try them." I pull out my phone and set it on top of the bar. Then bring up their website.

Lex leans in to see it better. "What are we looking for exactly?"

"Well, they have a website, so that's step one."

"I like how they've got the menu right on the home page."

"Yeah, that is smart," I agree.

Lex pulls out his phone and we huddle together, bouncing between screens. He brings up their social media pages while I look through their online reviews and ratings, and search through their online presence, including the Burlington tourism page. A food and wine vlog that did a feature on a Riesling that's only available here.

Lex's food comes and he eats while I compile some rough notes on the back of a napkin.

"You could use the notes app in your phone," he says around a bite of his burger.

"I think better with a pen and paper."

I'm finishing up when a deep voice starts crooning into the bar area. I swivel in my chair to face the stage in the corner.

"Killer first date, Kaitlyn. How'd you know I like live music?" Lex turns with me, his glass resting on his thigh.

"This isn't a date."

"Feels like one though, right?"

I roll my eyes. I'm focusing all of my efforts on reminding myself this is anything but a date.

The guy singing has a great voice and we listen through his first song. He gets a loud round of applause. He grins a little shyly, tips his salt and pepper head, and goes into his next song. A slower one that sets a mood over the bar.

"Wanna dance?" Lex asks.

"No." I turn back to face the bar. The bartender is nearby and judging by the smirk, I'm pretty sure he's enjoying watching me squirm on this non-date that feels a hell of a lot like a date.

"Suit yourself." Lex pushes out of his seat.

The spot next to me that he's been occupying for the last hour goes cold and quiet.

"He isn't?" I ask the bartender.

His gaze goes beyond me and he's got a ridiculously pleased grin. "Oh, he is."

Giving in, I look. He struts across the bar in his jeans and boots. A man in a hoodie shouldn't have that much confidence.

A couple of guys at a table in the middle of the bar stop him. Lex, charming as always, smiles and shakes hands.

"Looks like you're about to lose your boy to a man," the bartender says.

"He isn't gay."

"Me either, but as many times as you turned the poor guy down since you sat at my bar, might be enough to make him reconsider." He nods his head. "He can't dance, that's for sure."

He's moved from the table and stands in front of the stage. From across the room, he stares back at me while he sways side to side. Every head turns between us waiting to see what I'll do.

"Don't leave him hanging, honey," a burly guy in a trendy flannel shirt says. "Rainn, talk some sense into her."

"If I had a boyfriend that looked like that, I'd dance with him anywhere he wanted. Grocery store, parking lots, naked in our bedroom." Someone else adds. I don't look. My eyes are still locked with Lex's as he stubbornly holds his ground and moves his arms up to an imaginary person he's slow dancing with. He's ridiculous.

"He isn't my boyfriend," I insist.

"Song will be over soon," the bartender who I now know is definitely Rainn, says. "Don't miss your moment."

Oh for the love of annoyingly charming hockey players. It must be in my DNA. Something Dad slipped in to make my life more difficult. More lessons on hard work and discipline. Both fail me as I get to my feet. I should leave him here. Walk out the door and let him continue to make a fool of himself.

When I get to him, he has a pleased smile on his foolish face.

"I'm not dancing with you."

"You're always saying you're not going to do things. Isn't it exhausting constantly pushing against the flow?"

Yes.

"Come on. It's one dance. Less than that. The song is almost over." He takes advantage of my silence and grabs my hand, tugs me to him and places both hands at my hips.

"Everyone is staring." I can feel the weight of every eye in the place.

"Yeah, but they're staring at me."

I rest my hands on his shoulders. I'm pretty sure there's applause around the bar as I give in and dance with Lex.

"See? Not so bad." His fingers inch farther around my back, bringing me closer.

"You're actually not a bad dancer."

"A compliment at long last."

"And already I regret it."

"My mom taught me." His brown eyes sparkle in the dim lighting. "Three very painful nights before my first middle school dance in our living room where she coached me through slow dancing to nineties love ballads."

Laughter relaxes me under his touch. "I would have been glad to have danced with any boy in middle school who'd had a lesson or two."

"I never got the courage to ask anyone. Not that night anyway."

A self-conscious and timid Lex is hard for me to picture.

"You were probably in dance. Ballet? You've got one of those long necks and regal stares."

"I have a long neck?"

"Not freaky long. Like a ballerina."

"No, I was never in dance. I played hockey."

"Really?"

"Mhmm. Until I was thirteen."

"Why'd you quit?"

"It stopped being fun."

"What's your mom like?"

"My mom?" I ask, thrown by the question. People rarely ask about the non-famous part of my genetic makeup.

"You freeze up any time someone mentions your dad, so I figured your mom was a safer topic choice."

While it's true, I'm surprised he's noticed.

"She's beautiful and bubbly. My parents split when I was three and she moved to Seattle. The last time I talked to her, she was managing a local band."

"No shit?"

I nod. I'm pretty sure she's dating the guitarist, but I leave that part out. I stopped asking about her boyfriends years ago. They're all some sad, lesser version of my dad.

Don't get me wrong, the man makes me crazy. But he's a catch. Smart, successful, famous. And he doesn't look like my friend's dads wearing oversize button-down shirts and New Balance sneakers. Every teacher I had growing up hit on him in front of me. My friend's moms got all giggly and flirty around him. It was so embarrassing.

The guys my mom has moved on to have been upcoming artists or athletes as if she's hoping the next one will have a big break and she'll be the woman who was with him before the whole world fell in love with him.

I vowed that I'd never follow in either of their footsteps. I wouldn't be like my mom, chasing men who'd never love her as much as their careers nor would I be like my dad who gave so much to hockey and then his company that he simply didn't have enough space left in his heart for anything or anyone else.

"Did you shuttle between them growing up or…" Lex lets the question trail off.

"I'll give you one question. Just one, anything you want to know—within reason—about my dad, but that's it."

"You keep assuming it's him I want to know more about, but it's you."

The song ends and we stop swaying but don't step apart. I can't allow myself to believe him. History is the best decider of the future. Which means Lex can't be trusted—even if his words sound sincere.

"Let's get out of here," he says.

And I go because despite it all, I want to believe there's someone out there that thinks I'm enough all on my own.

LEX

We speed walk back to the hockey house, anxious to get out of the cold once again. When the old Victorian home comes into view, I tug her even faster toward the front entrance.

"Wait, wait." She stops suddenly and her hand pulls free. "I can't just walk in there. Come to my dorm instead."

"But we're already here."

She takes a step back. "This was a bad idea anyway. I don't know what I was thinking. I'll see you tomorrow."

"Come on. Don't go. We don't have to do anything. I just want to spend some more time with you."

She glances to the house behind me. "I don't want the guys on the team to know we're… hanging out."

Pax already knows and most of the others wouldn't blink an eye, but I get that it's more complicated since she's working for the team. "We'll go in through the back door."

Her lips twist into a smile and she quirks a brow. "Is that some sort of innuendo?"

I bark a laugh into the silent night. "Here's hoping."

Kaitlyn hides behind me as I step through the creaky back

entrance. It opens into the kitchen. "All clear," I whisper and hold the screen door wide for her.

"I'm just on the second floor. Almost there." I'm watching over my shoulder to make sure she follows and miss the first step. "Oh, fuck," I call out as I knock into the wall and hit my funny bone.

Kaitlyn giggles and then as if remembering where she is inhales sharply and holds her breath.

The TV is on in the living room, but I can't hear anyone in the house otherwise until Tate yells out, "Vonne, that you?"

"Yep, just me. Nobody else. All alone."

"Oh my god," Kaitlyn mutters quietly and she presses into me like she's trying to disappear.

"Up for some PlayStation?" he asks.

"Not tonight, pretty tired. Catch you tomorrow." I drag Kaitlyn behind me upstairs and into my room.

"We made it," I say as I shut us inside.

She starts giggling again. "How am I going to leave without being seen?"

"We'll deal with that later." I invade her space and wrap my arms around her back. "Or you might just be trapped forever."

I bring my mouth down near hers but not quite kissing her.

"I thought you just wanted to talk."

"I do… tell me everything about you."

"Later." She closes the distance, and her lips touch mine.

I don't waste one second kissing her back. For all her hesitation, when Kaitlyn gives in—she gives completely. She holds nothing back as her soft lips part. Our tongues tangle and teeth bump.

Cold fingers slide under my sweatshirt and the T-shirt underneath. My ab muscles contract under her touch. She pushes the material up exposing my lower stomach.

"Uh-uh," I say. "Gotta give me something first."

"Excuse me?" Her face pulls back, and those big, blue eyes search mine.

"You want this shirt, then you're going to have to earn it."

"What?" She laughs.

I flip on a lamp and then lean against the edge of the desk. "Do you want something to drink? I've got beer and Gatorade."

"I want you to take off your shirt and kiss me."

Finally having her admit out loud that she wants me is a boost, but I've got a sense of Kaitlyn. If we fool around tonight without talking, we'll be in the same place. She'll walk out of here pretending it was nothing.

I grab two beers and offer her one. "If you could have a superpower, what would you choose?"

"A superpower?" A smile splits her lips.

"It was the first question that came to mind." Probably because I'm using my super restraint to keep my dick from jumping up and slapping me for stopping to make idle conversation. "If you want me to take this off, you have to answer."

"An answer for an article of clothing?"

I nod and she steps forward and takes the beer from me.

"I'd want to fly."

"Fly?" I can't help but chuckle at a response I wasn't expecting. "No laser beam eyes to destroy your enemies?"

"Less effort and not as messy to just fly far away."

I open the beer and take a drink before setting it on the desk and pull off my sweatshirt, then run a hand through my hair as I toss the balled-up fabric at her.

She easily catches it. "If I ask you a question, do I have to take something off?"

"Up to you."

"Hmm."

"I'll give you a freebie." Moving to the bed, I sit and motion with my head for her to do the same. "I'd choose telepathy. Imagine how straightforward everything would be if we all knew exactly what other people were thinking."

"I guess so."

We sit knee to knee. She unravels the black scarf around her neck and drops it to the floor.

"Do you still play hockey at all?"

"Not in years. I've done my best to avoid it since I was a kid."

"Then why take a job as a hockey team's equipment manager?" The question is out as soon as I've thought it.

She waves for me to take something off, which I do—a boot.

"I needed a job, and it was that or changing diapers in the childhood education center. I took a chance that cleaning up your shit would be easier than the other."

"What's your dad think?"

Her eyes fall to her lap and I regret bringing him up. I wonder about him though and what it was like for her growing up as his daughter. What it's like now. But it really is just her I'm trying to understand.

"I haven't told him."

"So you're not close then?"

"It's complicated."

"I'm a pretty smart dude."

"We're different. He's never understood me or even tried to. We haven't been that close since I was little. He sent me to boarding school the first chance he got." I can see the pain on her face as she says it.

I go for a lighter question next. "Boarding school? What was that like?"

"Pretty cool. People didn't treat me weird there. My dad

was chump change. There was a girl on my floor who was an actual princess."

"People treated you weird before?"

"They treated me like the guys on the team do. You all see me, but you don't really see me at all. I'm not Kaitlyn, I'm Declan Dalager's daughter. And as soon as people realize I'm not their magic in with him, they lose interest in me."

"That's not true. At least not for me."

She shrugs out of her coat. "What are your parents like?"

Before I can answer, she holds up her beer. "Wait. Let me guess. Happily married, your mom is a teacher and your dad coached little league every summer?"

"Wrong. Parents are divorced. My dad owns a tire store and thinks baseball is about as exciting as hockey, and he sleeps through baseball games."

"Your dad doesn't like hockey?" she asks, shocked as she unzips the sides of her boots and drops them to the floor.

I pull her socked feet into my lap. "Sorry to burst the ridiculous family image you had for me."

"What about your mom?"

"She moved to Minnesota for a job when my parents split. Since then, I only see her once a year or so."

"I'm sorry."

"We talk on the phone every few weeks, so it isn't like I never hear from her. I should probably reach out to her more often instead of waiting for her to call. When she first left my dad, I was so pissed at her. He wanted to try to work on things and she didn't. Work hard and fight for what you want, that's something my dad drummed into my head at an early age. I'm not saying it would have made a difference, but love can't be that much different than anything else and hard work hasn't failed me yet."

Kaitlyn smiles. "That's such a you response. Now, are we done with the interrogations yet?"

"Not even close. I want to know all of it."

"Of what?"

"Your life story. Starting with what happened last Saturday outside of the Biscuit. Did I say something suave and amazing, or do you just have a thing for drunk dudes outside of bars?"

She smiles but it's a few seconds before she says, "My ex was there."

"At the Biscuit?"

"Mhmm. He and his new girlfriend were walking down the sidewalk toward us. I panicked. Sorry."

"I'm not. That kiss was hot."

She rolls her eyes. "You were so drunk I seriously doubt you could have told the difference."

She's absolutely wrong about that.

"Did you two end on bad terms or something?"

"Or something. He's dating my roommate."

"Ouch. I'm sorry he hurt you."

"We hurt each other." Her voice is soft, and she keeps her gaze downcast.

"I'm not sure that makes it any easier. When two guys collide hard on the ice, they usually both go down."

She nods.

From there, I take us back to happier conversation. We talk about our classes and lots of other random shit. Little by little, I'm able to get her to open up. And to get her mostly naked. Although that is only a side goal. We've kept it PG-13, but it's still been a blast hanging with her.

I like Kaitlyn. I like how tough she is, and I like that she isn't overly trusting, and that she doesn't share her stories with many people. It means that tonight I managed to break down some of those walls.

I can see that she's been hurt in the past and that it's made her jaded and untrusting. Maybe it's a romantic notion, but I want to give some of that trust back to her. Because she deserves that and because I can't stop thinking about her.

She sits up wearing only her black bra and leggings. "What time is it?"

I reach for my phone in my jeans pocket on the floor. "Almost two. Damn." I yawn as if my body's just now realized how tired I am. My early morning run is gonna be brutal.

"I need to get back."

"Stay."

"I don't think so."

"Why not?"

"Look, Lex, you seem to be a genuinely good guy and I had fun tonight, but I don't date hockey players. Especially now that I'm working for the team. It's too messy."

"How about kissing hockey players, do you do that?" I slide my arms around her waist and pull her down with me.

She palms my face and her thumb glides over the cleft in my chin. "It seems I do."

The air crackles around us. She shifts so she's fully on top of me and I take her mouth. Immediately my tongue sweeps in, tasting her. I cup her breasts through her bra and then slide the straps down from her shoulders so I can pull the material down.

Kaitlyn sits up and unclasps it. I lean with her and gently bite one nipple and then the other. Her eyes flutter closed. The only light is from the small lamp casting the room in a soft glow and shadows. She's so fucking beautiful. A goddess.

I kiss a path from her sternum to neck and then take her lips again. Softer this time. There's no need to rush. We've got all night.

"I think I like you, Kaitlyn."

"Yeah?" Her eyes open and she smirks then rubs herself along my painfully hard dick.

"These are fun." I palm her boobs again. The rosy buds tighten under my fingers.

"I'll give you the name of my doctor and you can get your own pair."

I let my hands fall to her hips and I guide her back and forth while lifting my hips to increase the friction. Fuuuck.

I flip her onto her back, which elicits another sweet giggle from her lips. It's cut off quickly when I place a kiss along the waistband of her leggings. Slim hip bones hold the material away from her lower stomach and I inch them down to reveal her panties. They're the same lacy black as her bra, and I'm super disappointed I didn't get to see the set together. Not disappointed enough to have her put on more clothes right now.

She helps me get her tight pants and panties off and then it's just Kaitlyn in all her naked glory laying on my bed.

"I changed my mind. I don't want to read minds. I want X-ray vision." I'm probably staring like an idiot, but Kaitlyn is fucking gorgeous. A naked girl is a naked girl. I would have mostly agreed with that statement until tonight.

Wrong. Kaitlyn is in a league all her own.

"Then I want to change mine too," she says, reaching for my boxers and pulling them down until my dick springs free. "I was going to say the ability to make things larger, but we're good."

Chuckling, I kiss her. My plan to take my time is swiftly thwarted when she wraps a hand around my dick and pumps me. I grab a condom from the desk drawer and cover myself. Her chest rises and falls with what I hope is excitement that matches my own.

I circle her clit with a thumb and then drop down to taste

her. She bucks and moans as I lick and suck her sweet pussy. I'm going to need more than one night. Way more than one time inside of her. I can already tell. We're both close with so little touching.

When I finally push inside of her, there's a collective groan as her body takes and squeezes me. I don't move until I'm sure I won't come immediately, but not moving is just as torturous. Adrenaline and lust surges through every cell and I feel lightheaded.

Just when I think I can't possibly be more turned on, her fingers circle the base of my cock and she squeezes. Stars dot my vision and I mutter a string of curses as I fight off being a one pump chump.

She's absolutely aware of the effect she has on me. A satisfied smile tugs at her lips. I pull out. "Turn over."

She complies and I line up again and push in slowly. With one hand on her lower back and the other at her hip, I rock into her.

I'm under no illusion that I'm in control but it's still satisfying as she falls apart beneath me.

Yeah, I'm definitely going to need more than one time. Way more.

We pass out in a tangle of limbs and blankets. When I wake, Kaitlyn is picking up her clothes off the floor. It's still dark out but I had enough sleep that my dick is wide awake. He doesn't need nearly as much sleep as I do.

"'Morning."

"Hey," she says without looking up.

"Come back to bed. It's early."

"I have to go. And this can't happen again." She pulls her

T-shirt over her head, which is a damn shame because waking up to Kaitlyn's perky boobs is a fantastic way to start the day.

I was prepared for this and have all sorts of reasons to contradict whatever excuse she comes up with. Exhibit A, *everything* about last night.

"Why not?"

"If the guys on the team found out, or the coaches… that wouldn't look good for me."

I sit up in bed. "I see your point, but come on, last night was pretty great. There's nothing in the rules about players and managers hooking up."

She doesn't argue but she keeps getting dressed.

"Let's hang out later today. What time are you done with classes?"

"Did you hear the thing I said about this." She motions between us, but she's smiling now. "Not happening again?"

Kaitlyn's default is always no. Honestly, I don't think she even lets herself entertain an idea before she adamantly shuts it down.

I swing my legs over the side of the bed and get to my feet. Her scarf is on the floor and I pick it up and drape it around her neck.

"You said you wanted me to try the five-eighths. Let's do that tonight."

"You want me to work extra? That's your play for getting me to spend more time with you?" She finishes putting on her coat and then buttons it.

"I'll help you fold laundry afterward."

"Yeah… no thanks. That's the opposite of helpful."

"Come on. It'll be fun. I can show off my awesome skating skills and then you can boss me around with whatever you need done—laundry, organizing, cleaning."

"It would be nice to have someone else spray down Kirk's pads." She scrunches up her nose.

"Done. Now get out of here before you change your mind."

She arches a brow.

"I'm kidding. Give me five and I'll walk you."

"No need. I don't need anyone seeing us together. Can you just make sure the coast is clear downstairs?"

"Yeah, in a minute," I say and pick her up and take her back to my bed.

KAITLYN

"I'm sorry about last night. Did you go anyway?" Vivian sits on my bed while I brush through my wet hair in the attached bathroom of my dorm room. My plan to get out of Lex's place early and shower before classes was thwarted by a whole lot of making out. I barely made it to my eight o'clock and then I had to sit through the next two hours smelling like sex.

"What?"

"Vino and Veritas. Did you go?" she asks again.

"Oh right. Yes, I went. How was study group?"

"Boring. So, what was it like? Did you see the hottie bartender?"

"Uhh." I turn away so she can't see my face. I'm pretty sure it has *I slept with a hockey player* written all over it. "The place was great. It has a really great vibe, and the drinks were amazing."

"And? Was hottie bartender there?"

"Yes, Rainn was working."

"Dammit. I'm so disappointed I missed him. If you tell me he tried to get your number, I'll be crushed."

"No, he definitely didn't. I don't think he's gay, though."

"Good. I wonder if he's on social media." She's quiet, scrolling through her phone, most likely stalking Rainn, while I finish my hair and makeup. We both have a break before our afternoon classes and then I have work. That's still so weird to say. In truth though, I'm not minding the few hours I spend at the rink every day.

I walk out of the bathroom holding a tube of mascara. Vivian glances up expectantly, I walk back to the bathroom, then turn around and come back. I really want to tell her about Lex. If nothing else, I just need to say it out loud to remind myself how crazy it was to go home with him. And who better to remind me of that than my best friend who hates hockey players with the passion of a thousand suns?

She looks at me, her brows drawn together. "What?"

"I need to tell you something."

"All right."

"You're not going to like it."

"O-kay. You're freaking me out." Setting her phone down on the comforter, Vivian gives me her undivided attention.

"I, sort of, hooked up with a hockey player."

She doesn't speak but her eyes widen.

"Lex invited himself along last night to Vino and Veritas, and we... whatever..." I wave the mascara, still in my hand, around. My life is officially batshit crazy.

"Wow. I..." She uncrosses her legs, goes silent again, and then gives her head a shake. "I wasn't expecting that. Do you like him or was this a one-off thing?"

Okay, a better response than I imagined. I expected Vivian to look more repulsed by the idea of hooking up with a hockey player. Then again, she's the one who constantly tells me how hot they are. Repulsive... but hot. And crap, I really need her to be repulsed and smack me back to reality because I am so, *so* not repulsed.

"At this point it'd be more like a three-off thing." My face heats like a teenager admitting her first crush.

"Three times?" She smirks. "Just last night?"

I nod. "I slept over."

"You haven't done a sleepover since Dylan. Wow."

"Wow? What does wow mean?"

"I'm just surprised is all. Not that you hooked up with him, but that you've got this whole look on your face right now like you did when you and Dylan first started dating. I thought he'd ruined this look for good." She points to my face.

"Lex is not like Dylan."

"No, he isn't." She shakes her head. "In fact, Lex isn't your type at all, which makes this so much more intriguing."

"Why isn't he my type? Because he's a hockey player?"

"Because he's into you."

"Ouch."

"I didn't mean it like that. Dylan was into you. Of course, he was. Most guys on this campus are into you. Dylan made you chase him. Just like you decided to go after the boring lacrosse player when you wanted to make Dylan jealous. And from the stories you've told me about Barnard, all of your exes fit the pattern. You like being the one to pursue *and* the one to bow out."

I don't like the sound of any of that as she lays it out so bluntly. "I didn't bow out with Dylan. He was clearly into Chastity and probably already hooking up with her." I don't actually know for sure if they did anything before we broke up, but I know he wanted to.

"You got out before he did. Or in case he did. Admit it, the only reason you hooked up with Snoozer, the boring lacrosse player, was because you wanted to force an out with Dylan?"

"His name is Snooder." Emmett Snooder. A really unfortunate name. But Emmett more than makes up for it in other aspects. Aspects I was happy to capitalize on to find out for sure if Dylan truly cared about me or not. "And, I'm not admitting that because it isn't true. I liked Dylan."

"I know you did." Vivian's voice softens. A soft speaking Vivian is a scary thing. She's all hard edges and tough love usually. "But you had one foot out the door the entire time. It was never going to work because you were always going to find a reason it couldn't."

She isn't wrong. I knew early on when I started dating Dylan that he liked Chastity. Even when he told me repeatedly that they were just friends. I think I might have realized it before he did. I pushed and pushed until I pushed them together.

"Well, my intuition was right about him." I wave toward Chastity's bedroom on the opposite side of our joined dorm room.

"Truth be told, I'm glad to see you dating someone that sees how great you are. Dylan and Snoozer didn't deserve you."

"We're not dating. It was a one-time… I mean, a three-time thing."

"If you say so, but he's pretty cute and aside from that whole fatal flaw of being a hockey player, Lex seems nice. Maybe he's different."

"He is nice."

"And different?"

"Everyone seems different until they're not."

"Well, keep your eyes open then, but have fun. I'm on standby if we need to ruin his life."

I chuckle. I'm not sure if Vivian's serious or not, but I wouldn't put anything past her.

During practices I hang by the sidelines and make the occasional equipment switch, refill water bottles, and basically anything else the team needs to keep practice running smoothly.

"Dalager," Coach Keller calls out during Tuesday's practice as I fix an edge on one of Tate's skates.

"Yeah, Coach?"

"Get a pair of skates on and help me out here." He turns back to the guys.

"Finished?" Tate asks. I've gone still with his skate still in my hand.

"Yeah, I think so. Let me know how it feels and I can take a look again after practice."

I trudge to the locker room and grab the smallest skates we have. I carry them out to the bench with shaky hands. Do I even remember how to skate?

I do. I know I do. I went ice skating last winter in New York, but this is different. Coach has the guys line up for their usual shootout drill, but this time he has them divide up into two teams. I slide my feet into the stiff boots. I lace them up as tight as I can and stand. They're a little big, but manageable.

When I step onto the ice, Coach Keller moves from his position at the blue line. "You stand here and make sure the next guy in line doesn't go until the guy before him touches the boards."

Coach Garfunkle is on the opposite end in charge of watching the same thing on the other side. Kirk and Josh are in the nets, and the Graham twins are first up in each of their respective teams.

Coach Keller lines up the five pucks for each team and then steps back with his whistle in hand. "Ready boys?"

Lex is on the team by me. In general, he does an impressive job of focusing on hockey during practices. Not that I'd expected him to suddenly be unable to focus on anything but me. I've never met a hockey player that cared about anything more than himself.

He glances up from the end of the line and smiles. For all my misgivings about getting involved with a hockey player, I don't think Lex is using me. Not outright. He's been sensitive to asking about my dad and I appreciate that more than he probably realizes. Who knows, maybe we can manage to have a good, sexy, fun fling. Last night was incredible and I'd like to do it again, but I meant what I said about not wanting the team to find out. I don't want to give them any reason to further scrutinize my actions.

When the whistle's blown, Patrick and Paxton skate hard to the pucks. Excited energy vibrates around the arena as the guys cheer on their teams. And in that excitement, I completely forget that hockey was ever not a part of my life or that I've hated it for years. I'm wrapped up in it just as much as them and equally disappointed when it's the other team who wins.

I'm in the equipment room after practice when Lex fills the doorway, still in his gear.

"Hey." I have the different blades for him to test. "Ready?"

"Actually, can I take a rain check? Paxton wants to work on some passing drills."

"Oh, yeah, of course. Less work for me." For reasons I can't understand, I'm disappointed.

"Sorry. It's just that Pax is offering his time and I need all the help I can get."

"It's fine."

"Wanna hang later?"

"Maybe. I'm not sure what my plans are." I have absolutely none, but I'm not going to be at his beck and call.

"All right. Well, how about I call you when I'm done and see if you're free?"

"Sure, whatever." I turn so that my focus is back on the pile of things I need to do before I can leave.

I don't hear him step forward, but his warm breath tickles the shell of my ear when he leans in. "Be free and I'll make it up to you."

I'm cleaning up my room and keeping myself busy while I postpone texting Lex back. He texted as soon as he was free to see if I wanted to hang out, but I'm making him sweat it out a bit more before I respond.

When my phone rings, I jump for it expecting Lex. *Dad.* Aside from a text that asked how my classes were going, I haven't heard from him since I started working as the equipment manager. Which has been nice because I'm not sure how I feel about telling him.

"Hey, sweetheart," he says when I answer. "How's it going?"

"Okay." I smooth out my comforter and fluff the pillows on my bed. "Just studying and picking up my room."

"Good. Glad to hear it. How are your classes?"

I roll my eyes. "They're fine, Dad. I'm making straight A's."

"All right, all right. I worry is all. I didn't keep track as well as I should have when you were at Barnard—"

"Dad, seriously. I'm doing fine." And I really am. The past two years at Barnard taught me a lot. Lessons I'm grateful for and others I'd rather forget.

"Okay," he says with a sigh. "What else have you been up to?"

"Nothing really. Classes, work..." I slap the back of my hand against my forehead. Well, I guess he knows I have a job now.

"A job?"

"Yes. It's part-time."

"Is it on campus?"

"It is."

"And it won't interfere with your studying?"

I bristle. Some part of me still wants his approval, even if I tell myself I don't need it. I think the thing that annoys me the most is knowing he'd never question my grades or time management if he knew I was working with the hockey team. Especially at his precious alumni.

"It won't interfere. My grades are fine."

"You said that when you were at Barnard too."

"It was one mistake and I've already apologized for disgracing the Dalager name."

He sighs. "I didn't call to argue."

"Then why did you call?"

"To see how you were doing and to let you know that I'm coming to Burlington at the end of the month."

"For what?"

"You mean besides to see my daughter?"

I don't respond and get another giant sigh. "Dalager Sports attends the career fair every year. My assistant and I are flying down Friday morning and I'm going to stay through the weekend."

"Are you going to the game?" I bite my lip. "The hockey game, I mean. Assuming there is one."

"There is, although I'm surprised you know."

"It's hard not to know here. Besides, don't they play every weekend or something?"

He chuckles. "Moo U is definitely a hockey school. I don't know that I'll have time to make a game, but I might stop by and see Coach Keller."

Crap. There's no way I'll be able to hide my job if he talks with Coach.

"Anyway, the career fair is the week before Thanksgiving. Can you fly back to New York with me for break? We could leave as soon as your classes are done for the week."

"I know when the career fair is, Dad. I'm actually interviewing with Hawthorne for a marketing internship this summer."

"Hawthorne," he says. "Good company. We used them last year for a web campaign."

I saw the campaign. They did a great job.

"Anyway, I think I'm going to have to stay for Thanksgiving break. For my job."

"Oh." He sounds surprised and I fidget while holding the phone to my ear. "Well, I could shuffle some things and stay in Vermont so we're together at least."

"That really isn't necessary."

"It's as good as done."

"Really?" A little sprout of hope mixed with a lot of nerves takes root in my stomach.

"Don't sound so surprised. I've missed you."

A knock at my door gets my attention and I'm thankful for an excuse to get off the phone. Hope is a dangerous animal to feed. "I've gotta go."

"All right. Call if you need anything."

"Yep, I will. Bye." The knocking at my door continues. I hang up before Dad can respond, toss my phone on the bed, and hurry to the door.

Lex is on the other side with a lopsided grin. "Hey. I wondered if you were going to make me stand out here all night groveling."

"You can grovel inside," I say as I grab him by the hand and tug him into my room.

LEX

"How did you end up in Vermont?" I ask after I've appropriately groveled by giving her two orgasms. "I know your dad went here and I think we're working on making you a Moo U hockey fan, but…"

"Choose your next words carefully, Vonne. You're still naked."

I chuckle and bring my left arm behind my head so I can better see Kaitlyn. Her face is resting on my stomach.

"Why Vermont?"

"My dad suggested it and I didn't fight him." She shrugs one shoulder. "I just wanted to finish college."

"Are you ever going to tell me why you left your last school?"

"I'm sure you could ask your buddies and they'd tell you everything you need to know."

"I don't want their version. I want yours."

She looks up. "I was kicked out for cheating. A bunch of us were. It's a long story."

"I have all night."

"I can think of a lot better ways to spend the time."

"Always so quick to change the subject when you're in the hot seat."

Her fingernail makes little circles on my chest. She doesn't look at me as she speaks. "The short version is that I was enjoying college a little too much and got behind in a philosophy class. A friend of a friend had the test, he emailed it around, and we got caught. My dad flipped out and here I am, banished to Vermont."

"I'm sorry."

She shrugs. "I don't always make the best choices."

It seems like that statement is about more than cheating on a test, but I let it go.

"Do you actually play that thing?" I point to the guitar resting against the wall across the room.

She lifts her head. "Yeah, and I'm good at it too."

"Play me something."

"Now?"

"You can hop back on my penis if you want, but I remember someone saying she needed a break for her *lady parts*." I air quote the last two words and cringe a bit as I repeat the phrase.

She gets up and grabs the guitar and takes a seat at the end of the bed. I sit up and enjoy the view. Crossed legs, guitar resting in her lap, naked limbs, sex hair—Kaitlyn with a guitar is way sexier than I imagined when I brought it up.

She strums a little, eyes downcast. "What do you want me to play?"

"Anything."

Her picking gets more intentional and the music more recognizable. I can't quite put my finger on it, but I know that it's a song I've heard before.

"You're really good." And she is. I assumed she played guitar in the same way other people I've known do. They can play one song, maybe two. And even those are rough versions that don't sound much like the original. Nothing like the sure and pleasant melody Kaitlyn plays.

It's dark and haunting and I have chills when she finally starts singing along. Her voice is incredible, too. I'm starting to wonder if there's anything this girl can't do.

When she finishes, she looks up and a shy smile tugs at her lips. That sure and cocky girl stripped down and vulnerable.

I must look as dumbstruck as I feel. My heart's in my throat and I can't figure out one single thing to say.

"What? Was it bad? I haven't played that one in a while."

"Damn, Kaitlyn, that was amazing."

A small smirk tips up the corners of her mouth. "That's my dad's favorite. It was the first song I learned to play."

"Pink Floyd is badass."

She sets the guitar down on the floor and I pull her to me.

"Not as badass as you, though."

Over the next two weeks my days look a lot like this: wake up early to work out, go to classes, practice, extra skills with Pax any time he's free, and then spend the night tangled up with Kaitlyn. Somewhere in between all that I manage to eat and study.

Saturday night after another win, the guys are in good spirits. I am too. I got a chance to play on the third line when Ash took a puck to the knee and sat out for the second and third periods. His bad luck was good for me, but he'll be back next weekend and I'll more than likely be back on that fourth line. But for tonight, I'm going to enjoy it.

For once, I'm the first one showered and ready to go.

"See you boys in a few," I say with my bag on my shoulder.

On the way out, I stop by to see Kaitlyn. "Hey, we're having a party at the house."

"I heard." She's putting sticks back up on the wall and doesn't turn around to face me.

"See you in a bit?"

"I'm not sure." She glances back. "I promised Vivian we'd hang out. I haven't seen her much this week."

I can't help the grin that tugs at my lips because the reason she hasn't seen Vivian is because she's been with me. Not that I want to keep her from her friend, but I like that she's as caught up in spending time together as I am. She's far more fun than I ever imagined. And deep. I don't know. There's just something about her that makes me want to spend hours talking and hanging out, getting naked.

"Bring her."

She laughs. "I doubt very much that Vivian is walking into the hockey house in this lifetime."

I step into the room and place a hand at her hip, looping my finger over the waistband of her jeans. Her skin is smooth and warm. "Come on. It'll be fun."

Her gaze drops to my hand and she steps away. She lowers her voice. "I don't want the team to know we're hooking up."

I raise my hands. "I'll keep my paws to myself."

"Yeah, right."

"I will try my best." Because damn if it isn't hard not to when she's around.

"I don't think it's a good idea. I need this job."

"All right. I get it. Would it help if we talked to Coach and told him we were dating?"

Her eyes get wide.

"I'll take that as a no."

"I'm not ready for that, Lex, but maybe I can come over later?"

I should be excited about that because hello, sex, but this isn't just a hookup for me. I want to hang out with her at parties and bars, with our friends. I want to date her.

"Sure, whatever." I head for the door, feeling more than a little discouraged. "Text me later."

Two hours later, I'm sitting in the living room with Paxton and Jonah. The guys are talking about the game, which would normally be my favorite topic of conversation, but I'm distracted wondering what Kaitlyn is up to and who she's hanging with, if she'll come by later.

"You looked good out there," Paxton says. "Has Coach said anything about moving you to the third line permanently?"

"Nah, he—" I lose my train of thought when the door opens, and Kaitlyn pauses at the threshold with Vivian. She doesn't see me right away, but she scans the room and I like to think she's looking for me.

She changed since the game. She's wearing tight jeans and tall boots that come over her knees. She's got her coat on, but it's unbuttoned. The black sweater hits her midriff, showing off her stomach. Today she's got a yellow scarf that makes her blue eyes stand out.

"Vonne? Hellooo?" Pax waves a hand in front of my face.

"Good. Yeah, I feel good."

Kaitlyn finally spots me, and I lift a hand to wave. She smiles, waves, but then walks toward the back of the house. Vivian gives me a friendly glare. I think I'm slowly winning her over. Very slowly.

I snap my attention back to the guys. "What were you saying?"

They laugh.

Pax shakes his head. "What's your deal with Kaitlyn?"

"I don't know. She's fascinating."

"She's trouble," Jonah states implicitly. "Hot trouble, but definitely trouble."

"I can handle her."

"You sure about that?" Pax asks.

I don't think she's as tough as she lets on, but I doubt saying that to the guys would win me any points with her. I stand. "I'm sure."

I start toward her, but hear Jonah call after me, "Better double-check your shit every day just in case."

She's talking with Patrick when I get to the kitchen. He hands her a cup and then Vivian.

"Thank you for the empty cup." Kaitlyn holds it in front of her.

"Keg's out back." Pat tips his head toward the yard.

"Do you live here?" Vivian asks him.

"Nah," I interrupt. "None of the rooms were big enough for his ego."

"Hey." I lightly bump shoulders with Kaitlyn and then jut my chin to Vivian. "You guys came."

"It took some convincing." Patrick leans against the counter. "They were going to the lacrosse house instead. Those dudes are lame."

Kaitlyn glances at me. "We planned to bounce around a few parties, but you guys were very convincing."

"Let's get you ladies a drink," Pat says and turns his hat backward.

Vivian follows him to the door. Kaitlyn hangs back a second. "I'll see you later, okay?"

Nodding, I let her go. Guess we won't be hanging out.

I head out back too, but instead of following Kaitlyn, I go over to where Ash and some of the guys are standing around the fire pit. For the next couple of hours, I find myself getting more and more frustrated. Why the hell can't we hang out at a party? She can hang out with everyone else but me?

I'm trying to be sensitive to her feelings and I know she doesn't want to throw it in everyone's face, but no one gives a flying fuck if we stand together at a party. It's bullshit and it makes me feel like I've been tossed on her fourth line.

She and Vivian are near the keg and I head there to refill my cup. Patrick is still with them.

Kaitlyn looks up and smiles when I get close. A smile that tells me she wants to be hanging with me, which in turn just makes me more frustrated and determined to do just that.

"You ready then, Dalager?" Pat asks.

"This I have to see," Vivian says excitedly.

"See what?" I ask, looking around.

"Kaitlyn here thinks she can beat me at washers," Patrick says with a slow shake of his head.

My girl doesn't back down. No shocker there. Her shoulders straighten as she stands tall. "I don't think. I *know*."

Patrick is arrogant and usually rightfully so. He's the best at just about any games we play. He finishes off his beer. "Let's see it then."

I grab Kaitlyn's wrist to slow her before she leaves me again. "Hey."

"Hey," she parrots with a smirk and pulls free. "Ready to see me kick his ass?"

"He's pretty good."

"So am I."

Patrick grabs the washers, hands Kaitlyn hers, and moves back to the opposite side.

"Ladies first," Patrick says and waves for her to go ahead.

"Is she any good?" I ask Vivian while Kaitlyn lines up and prepares to throw her first washer.

"I have no idea, but if I know my girl, she wouldn't make a dare she couldn't win. I hope she destroys him."

I chuckle. "Of course you do." Then I take a step back from her. She does have beer in her hand after all.

Kaitlyn pitches her first washer, and we watch as it sails through the air, hits the rim of the hole, and then bounces out of the box.

Patrick whistles and shakes his head. He tosses his first washer, and it lands inside the box.

A crowd starts to form as the two battle it out. Kaitlyn's good but Patrick maintains his lead, capitalizing any time Kaitlyn misses.

We all want to see Patrick get beat. He's a likable guy—always up for a good time but serious when he steps out onto the ice—but still, seeing Kaitlyn put up a decent fight against him has us cheering her on as it comes down to the final toss. Patrick needs one more point, so he only needs to get it into the box. If Kaitlyn misses, she loses. The only way she can win is to get it into the hole. Something she's only managed once all game.

Pat pitches his and it hits the back of the box and narrowly misses the hole, ending up in the front of the box. "That's game," he calls with a smug smile.

"Not so fast," Kaitlyn says. "Don't count your chickens before they're hatched."

"Bock, bock." He laughs.

Kaitlyn blows out a breath and holds the washer out in front of her, lining up and then pitching it. I fucking hold my breath like it's the world championship.

The yard explodes with cheers as her washer lands square in the hole. Patrick's jaw drops. "What?! No way! No way!" He takes off running around the yard screaming like an idiot.

I start to walk over to Kaitlyn. She's got a victorious and

amused look on her face. A couple of the guys rush her before I get there and hoist her up on their shoulders, chanting her name.

"Nice game," I shout up to her. She smiles down at me as the guys move with her around the yard.

Patrick finally completes his lap of defeat and stops in front of me, out of breath. "She beat me."

"I saw."

"Fuck." He slaps me on the shoulder. "Guess it's time to drink. I'm good sober, but drunk, I'm unbeatable. Rematch in thirty."

When the guys finally drop her, Kaitlyn wanders over to me.

"You've officially won over the team."

She chuckles. "They're drunk."

"I'm glad you came."

"I wasn't sure if I should, but Patrick invited me, and Vivian wanted another opportunity to throw a beer in someone's face."

"Patrick convinced you?"

She nods. "Yeah." Then adds, "I mean, no. It isn't like that."

"What's it like?"

"I couldn't show up here tonight as your... whatever. But since he invited me, it was less complicated."

"The guys don't care who you're hooking up with. Plenty of the guys have girlfriends. Besides, I'm not talking about making out in front of everyone, I just want to hang out at a party with a chick I really like being with."

"People will know. They'll figure it out. You're not exactly subtle."

"I don't give a shit about people running their mouths on things they *think* they know. I like you. I think you're cool as hell, but I won't be the guy that you hook up with when there's no better option but pretend doesn't exist all the rest of the time."

"You know that isn't what I meant," she argues. "I came here tonight to see *you*."

"You have a funny way of showing it."

She steps an inch closer. "I like you too, Lex. I didn't want to, but I do. I'm here for you. I'm sorry if it doesn't seem that way."

"Wow. I feel all warm and fuzzy. You didn't want to like me?"

She rolls her eyes. "You're twisting everything I say. I just think it puts me in a weird spot with the guys if I show up here as your girl, or whatever. We haven't even talked about what it is we're doing and you're acting like you need to claim me in front of your buddies to prove something."

"Should I leave my bedroom door unlocked tonight or does that also put you in a weird spot?" I'm aware that I'm trending toward unreasonable, but damn, it hurts to have her put up these arbitrary rules between us. I don't want to only be able to talk to her or touch her behind closed doors. And it isn't about claiming her. It's about experiencing things with her.

"If that's not what you want anymore, then I understand."

"What I want is to not play games, Kait. Or worry about when I can and can't touch you. You like me or you don't. You want to be with me or you don't. It's really that simple."

"Lex," she starts but I walk off saving myself from hearing more of her excuses.

KAITLYN

"He looks like you kicked his dog." Vivian is staring at Lex across the yard. We both are. He's in a circle of guys and Jonah is telling a story that has the rest of them doubled over in laughter. Everyone except Lex.

"He's being ridiculous."

"Maybe." Her tone tells me she doesn't think so.

I shoot her a glare.

"You did come over to the guy's house and proceed to spend the night hanging out with another dude. One you're not even interested in."

"It's a party. Besides, I'm not his property. We're just hooking up."

"So, if he decided to take someone else up to his room later, you'd be totally okay with it?"

White hot jealousy courses through my veins. I'm not an idiot. I know there are lots of girls that would jump at the opportunity. I see the way people look at him. He's ridiculously hot and he's charming and nice. Ugh. Even now there's a group of girls hanging near him and I know if I were to walk out of here tonight, he'd have no problem finding a girl or three to take upstairs.

"Ha!" She points at my face. "I didn't think so."

"Still. What am I supposed to do? Go over there and hang on him all night like I'm some pathetic girl hoping he'll bring me upstairs later."

"Would that really be so bad? The pathetic part aside. You know you aren't pathetic. He knows you're not pathetic." Vivian shrugs. "Finding a guy I want to hang on, is the sole reason I go to parties. I would way rather a night in, but sadly there are no boys there."

"Really?"

"Yeah. I don't need a reason to get dressed up. My shoes are just as fabulous at home as they are here."

I glance down at her five-inch stiletto boots. They are fabulous.

"Well, there are plenty here." I motion with my cup.

"Hockey boys. Bleh."

"You know, they aren't all bad."

"You mean like Lex?" She smiles and bats her eyelashes innocently.

"Since when did you start taking his side."

"I'm always on your side, but sometimes you're wrong and need someone to point it out."

I laugh and she squeezes my arm. "Go."

"What about you?"

"I'm fine. I think I'll go grab another drink. Patrick might need some consoling after that beating you gave him. Or maybe I'll see if I can find that guy, Ash. Did you see his arms?"

"You know he's a hockey player, right?"

She waves me off. "If he mentions the H word, I'll just toss a drink in his face."

I take my time walking across the yard. Lex smiles as Jonah continues, but in that way people do when they're just being polite and don't really mean it.

Oh, god, am I really going to out myself in front of the entire team?

I'm not ashamed to be hooking up with Lex. He's hot and nice and the sex is beyond. And the guys probably won't care, Lex is right, but… making a gesture like this means something to Lex. I know it does. I can read it all over his handsome face.

The last time I dated someone, it blew up in my face. I can't take another blow this year. I just can't. But, I don't want to lose him either. Despite all my misgivings, he makes me feel seen. Vermont feels less like a punishment since I've started hanging out with him. Which means, we're about to go from quietly hooking up to dating. I'm dating a hockey player. In what world did I allow that to happen? I can't help but feel like I'm voluntarily walking into the fire.

Lex glances up and meets my gaze and then quickly looks away. I don't think simply walking up and standing at his side is going to cut it. I'm going to have to make it clear to him, and everyone else, that he's my guy.

When I'm just about to Lex and his group, Patrick steps in front of me. "Dalager, I need a rematch."

"Oh no. I'm retired."

"Quitting while you're ahead. Smart. I should try that more." He darts off.

I continue walking toward the group of guys, but now Lex isn't there. I do a quick scan of the yard finally finding him on his way back inside the house.

"Yo, Vonne," I yell over the music and hum of conversation.

He pauses with his hand on the door and looks over his shoulder. "Yeah?"

I hurry to him. My heart is galloping in my chest every step of the way. I slow when I get to the bottom step.

"Something I can help you with?" He almost smirks. I know he's thinking I want to go upstairs to his room. I do. I really, really do. Public grand gestures are so not my style. Being with him is so much simpler when it's just the two of us.

Since I can't think of what to say, I don't speak at all. I go to him and wrap my arms around his neck and kiss him. He chuckles in surprise but then his lips claim mine back. His hands move to my hips and suddenly I've lost all control of this moment.

A few catcalls come from behind us and a couple people cheer him on, but when we finally break apart the world hasn't stopped like I feared. The music still pumps, and people go back to drinking and chatting like two people making out in the middle of the party is no big deal. I guess it really isn't if you're one of them, but I still feel like an outsider.

I like these guys. For the most part, they're a really good, fun group. I've never hated hockey players like Vivian. I've avoided the hockey world, which in turn has meant hockey players, but now that I'm around it again I don't want to screw it up. I'm actually enjoying my job and I'm pretty good at it.

"You realize everyone just saw that, right?" he asks with a grin and starts to drop his mouth back to mine.

I put a hand up to stop him. "That was the point. Just so you know, though, I'm not this girl. The one who is going to stand by your side all night long and smile and giggle at whatever you say."

He barks out a laugh. "No shit, baby doll."

"And that pet name is gonna have to go."

"Sure thing, *baby doll*." With a huge grin, he kisses me again. "Wanna go upstairs?"

"Later. I have an idea."

After finding Vivian and Ash, the four of us play a few games of washers and then eventually move inside when the cold becomes too much. I'm sitting next to Lex on the couch, his arm is casually draped behind me.

"I think I'm going to grab a ride home. Are you coming, Kait?" Vivian asks.

She and Ash have been flirting but as far as I can tell neither has made a move. I can hardly blame Ash, or any of these guys, since they're well aware of her grudge against hockey players. I glance at Ash to see his reaction to her leaving. He looks down to his beer as she stands.

"I'm going to stay," I tell my best friend.

She grins. "Okay. Call me tomorrow."

Ash moves to his feet. "Let me walk you out."

Tate and his girlfriend Maggie stand as well. "We're going to bed, too. 'Night all," Tate says. Maggie waves.

Jonah and Patrick are playing video games. Patrick has a girl sitting beside him, but the three of them aren't paying any attention to Lex and me.

"Come with me." Lex stands and helps me to my feet. "I want to show you something."

He leads me through the kitchen toward the attached dining room. Cups and a few empty liquor bottles litter the countertop. Shot glasses and beer cans set on the old wood table where earlier people were playing cards and quarters.

"This table has been handed down a bunch of generations. It has names of guys that played dating all the way back to the eighties." Sure enough, there are names scribbled in ink and Sharpie all over. Some are just names, some include the year or their jersey number. In the middle, someone drew an impressive bull mascot in green and black.

"This is really cool. Where is your name?"

"I haven't put mine on it yet."

"Why not?"

"I'm not sure. I started to a couple times, but it feels like a much bigger deal than just scribbling my name in some random spot. Years and years of names. I memorized them all. Looked up the ones I didn't know. Some of the guys went on to do big things in the hockey world and others didn't but they're all here together as this sacred thing. I guess I don't feel worthy yet." He grins sheepishly. "I'm romanticizing it, I know. The guys already gave me shit about it."

"No, I get it. It's a really cool thing to be a part of."

He nods and squeezes my hand, then uses his other to point to a signature on the table.

Declan Dalager. #11

My dad. His penmanship hasn't changed but seeing it here with the others feels surreal. It's hard to imagine him here just like Lex, and the rest of the guys. All the great things that still lie ahead of him.

"I know you don't like it when I bring up your dad, but I thought you'd want to see."

"Thank you for showing me." I run my finger below it.

"Of course." He pulls me to him and kisses me quick.

"Wanna go back outside?" I ask him. A decent number of people are still out in the yard sitting around drinking next to a fire pit.

"No. My toes are just now thawed out from earlier." He laughs. "Are you really staying over?"

"Unless you have other plans?"

"Couple chicks coming by later, but I'll cancel." He winks and tugs me toward the stairs.

He doesn't bother turning on the light in his room. His lips find mine and his fingers disappear underneath the hem of my sweatshirt. Calloused fingertips and big palms travel over my hips and up to the curve of my waist.

I pull up his shirt, and he breaks away long enough to take it off and toss it on the floor. In the dark I can't see much of his abs and chest, but Lex has a great upper body. Lean and sculpted, smooth muscles that are the perfect size.

Running my hands up his pecs to his shoulders and then down over his biceps, I'm greedy with my touch before I move to unbutton his jeans. His hands return to exploring my sides. He's much more patient than I am.

I push his jeans and boxers down far enough that I can get my hand down and take his dick out. Long and thick and so very hard. He hisses out a breath as I stroke him.

"Fuck, Kait. Slow down."

But I'm in no mood for slow tonight. I kneel and take him in my mouth. Laughter dies on his lips as I swirl my tongue along the tip and then suck him to the base. I glance up at him as I pop off.

"You were saying?"

With a smirk, he guides my head back to his cock. I open wide and let him guide me over his length.

I'm just really getting into it as he mutters a string of curses and guttural moans. He steps back and swoops me up, lays me on the bed, and his mouth covers mine. I'm still fully dressed but damn if I don't feel more turned on than I ever have before.

"Do they match?" he asks as his lips move to my neck.

"What?"

"Your bra and panties. Do they match again? I keep forgetting to fully appreciate the effort."

"Yes."

He hops to his feet and I'm flung up beside him. Lex has a freaky strength, tossing me around like it's nothing. Slowly, he lifts my sweater over my head. His dark eyes hone in on my red bra. He seems a little transfixed, so I unbutton my jeans, revealing the top of my matching panties.

He kneels in front of me, unzips my boots and helps me out of them, then together we remove my jeans. There's something about the way Lex undresses me. As if he were unwrapping a lone present under the Christmas tree, taking his time and carefully peeling back the tape so he doesn't rip the paper. Controlled and deliberate.

His hands slide over my legs and he kisses the inside of my thigh. Lifting one leg, he brings it up to his shoulder and suctions his lips over my pussy.

My legs tremble as he slips a finger underneath the lacy material and shoves it to the side so he can taste me.

Once again, I'm hoisted and moved to the bed where he continues to lick and suck without removing my panties, just moving them to the side out of his way.

My first orgasm builds and then catches me by surprise with how quickly Lex gets me over the edge. He keeps on sucking and adds a finger, coaxing a second orgasm that brings tears to my eyes as pleasure explodes behind my eyelids.

"I think I'm gonna die if you keep doing that," I say as his mouth stays focused on my pussy.

Through his laughter, he kisses a trail up to my belly button. He grabs a condom from the desk and covers himself, then stares down at me. "You're so goddamn beautiful."

Slowly, he slides my panties down my legs, then sits and pulls me carefully onto his lap and I sink down onto him slowly. Stretching and filling me so tight.

Staring into my eyes, his gaze is playful and sexy. I could live a thousand lives and still be thinking about the consuming way he looks at me now.

He fights his release until I'm close again. I don't know

how many orgasms this guy could coax out of me but as the third one washes over me, my limbs go limp and I slump onto him breathless and sweaty.

"No more," I mumble into his shoulder.

"You say that now, but in five minutes you'll change your mind."

And he's probably right. I'm totally addicted.

LEX

Kaitlyn sits across from me at the coffeehouse. She's tapping away on her computer, pen between her teeth. We're supposed to be studying but only one of us is accomplishing it. I'm distracted. It's my new thing, apparently. Even when she's not around, I find myself thinking about her—remembering something she said or did.

She looks up and catches me staring. Her brows raise and an amused smile tugs at the corner of her lips. "You're supposed to be studying."

"I am."

"Studying English lit, not me."

"You're more interesting." If Kaitlyn were a class, I'd be acing it for sure.

She laughs. "If your grade slips, you won't play."

Fuck, she's right. I straighten in my chair and pull up the study questions. The weekly quizzes are kicking my ass. I do all the reading, but my eyes glaze over for most of it. Sitting still to read anything has never been my thing. Still, I'm managing to keep decent grades so far.

"How's your marketing project coming, the Vino and Veritas one?"

"Good. I had to submit the idea with notes and an outline. The professor loved it. Now I just need to finish typing up my analysis and recommendations. I think I'm going to use it for my interview with Hawthorne Marketing at the career fair."

"What do you want to do when you graduate?"

"You need to read," she says with a smile.

"Yeah, yeah. I will."

"*If* I get an internship with Hawthorne, then I'm hoping I'll have an in after graduation. They're the best marketing firm in Boston."

"Huh." I try to picture her in a big office in a downtown building.

"What?"

"Nothing, I guess I'm surprised you don't want to work with your dad. They have a marketing department, yeah?"

"Yes, but there's no way I'm working for him. I haven't been inside Dalager Sports headquarters in years. Besides, you don't want to work with your dad either."

"That's different. I might want to if it had anything to do with hockey." I shut my book. Let's be honest, I'm not getting any studying done right now. "What's your deal with him anyway? Was he a shit dad?"

"No," she says quickly and then her mouth pulls into a tight line. "We're just not close, okay?"

I really want to know more so I can understand where all the animosity comes from, but her tone is clear that this isn't open for discussion, so I nod. "Okay."

Later that afternoon, I get her on the ice with me while I test out the five-eighths radius. The twins and Jonah stayed, too, and we run some light drills. Kaitlyn hangs by the side, observing.

"What do you think?" she asks as I skate up to her.

"You were right."

She leans closer with a smug smile. "I'm sorry. What was that?"

I take her hand and pull her out farther onto the ice. "Let's see what you got, Dalager."

I pick up my stick and hand it to her. The guys stop and Pax sends an easy pass to her while I go and grab another stick from the bench. She stops the puck and adjusts her grip.

I hang off to the side while I watch her take a shot that slides in on the right side of the net.

Patrick pulls it out and sends it back to her, but this time I get in front of her.

She skates left and passes it to Pat. Pax strips it from his brother and shoots it up to me. I'm in total show-off mode as I dribble the puck side to side and then front to back. I send the puck through her legs to Pax who makes an easy shot into an open net.

Her eyes narrow in annoyed defeat. I grab her by the waist and kiss that glare away.

She pushes at my chest. "Again. I want another chance. And no taking it easy on me."

"You need a helmet, young lady," I tell her. "And some pads."

"Let's do a shootout," Pax says. "Lex versus Kaitlyn. Best of five from the blue line."

"Done," she says quickly.

"You agreed to that awfully fast."

Pax snorts. "She's seen you play."

"Ladies first, then."

We move out of her way and Kaitlyn skates with the puck to the blue line. She takes her time, staring ahead at the goal with a sexy look of intense determination. Her first attempt goes wide to the left. She readjusts her grip, and I can see the deep breath she takes with the lift and fall of her shoulders.

On the exhale, she shoots, and this time it sails beautifully down the center of the ice and into the goal. She raises her arms overhead with the stick still in her hand. I've never seen her look so happy.

And I realize she doesn't hate hockey. Not one bit. She loves it. She loves it so much she hated it to protect herself. If hockey weren't part of my life anymore, I'd probably pretend to hate it too.

It's the same way she pretends to not care about her crappy relationship with her dad. She absolutely cares. So much that the only way she can get through the day is to block it. I can't believe I didn't see it earlier.

"Where are we going?" she asks as I help her into Tate's beat-up truck.

"I'm taking you to dinner."

"You don't need to do that, Lex. Neither of us has cash to blow."

"I'm a poor college kid, but I'm not destitute, and I want to take my girl to dinner."

Through a small laugh, she relents. "Fine, but I've got dessert."

"You are dessert, baby doll."

I start up the truck and take us to downtown Burlington, then around some of the outskirts. The radio is on and she sits close enough that I can rest my right hand on her thigh. Her tight leggings are this velvety material that I can't stop touching.

"Uhh, Lex, are we going in circles?" she asks as we get back to the downtown area.

Chuckling softly, I grin at her. "We're almost there."

When I pull up back in front of the hockey house, she shoots me a confused look. "I don't understand."

I shut off the engine and get out, round the truck, and open her door. "I made you dinner."

"You cook?" Her blue eyes widen with disbelief.

I help her down and we walk toward the house. "Not many things, but I make a mean Italian feast."

The spaghetti sauce is simmering on the stove and the rest of the ingredients are laid out on the countertop.

"Have a seat, my lady," I tell her as I push up my sleeves.

"You're too much. Why did we drive around for an hour?"

"The guys were cleaning up," I admit. "I hope you like spaghetti."

I pour her a glass of wine. She sips and leans against the countertop. "I do and it actually smells good."

"Don't be so surprised. I have many talents." I crowd her so she's trapped between me and the counter, place my hands on either side of her, and take her mouth. If I don't focus, this dinner could turn out with me feasting on her instead. And I promised my girl dinner.

"Tate helped," I admit as I step back. "But, the garlic bread was all me."

"You mean you took it out of a bag and put it in the oven?"

"Yep." I give an exaggerated chef's kiss that makes her laugh.

We talk while I keep an eye on the food. A few of the guys

are in the living room, but they stay out of the kitchen and it's easy for me to ignore them with Kaitlyn nearby.

"I think these are done," I say as I test a noodle.

She takes one and throws it against the wall above the stove. "Seems so."

"What was that?" I ask, pointing to where a single spaghetti noodle sticks to the wall.

"That's how you can check if spaghetti is done. If it sticks, it's done. If it doesn't, then it needs to be cooked longer."

"Are you pulling my leg?"

"No!" She laughs and her cheeks pink. "It's true."

"Dare I ask where you learned this absolutely ludicrous technique?"

"My dad." She hides behind her wine glass. "Then again, his idea of home cooked was reheating food some assistant or cook had made for us."

"I'm always sticking my foot in my mouth. I'm sorry." It seems like no matter how hard I try to avoid conversations about her dad, we end up here.

"You couldn't have known."

"You can talk to me. You know that, right? Even if it's just to get it off your chest."

"I do. Thank you."

When it's clear she's not ready to get anything off her chest right now, I nod. "All right. Let's eat."

I've no more than pulled everything together and handed Kaitlyn a plate when Jonah peeks into the kitchen. "What's that smell?"

"Food that's not for you," I tell him as I lead Kaitlyn into the dining room. I found some candles and a mostly-not-stained tablecloth to set the mood.

She swirls the noodles around a fork and dips her head

close to her plate to take a bite. I swear this girl makes the most ridiculous things look sexy.

"This is really good, Lex."

I take a big bite out of the garlic bread and nod my agreement.

Whispering in the kitchen gets my attention and I lean back in my chair to see the twins staring at the food on the stovetop.

"Can I help you?" I ask, mouth partially full so it comes out a little mumbled.

"Just wondering if you're going to eat all of this," Pax says.

"Yes," I say at the same time Kaitlyn says, "No way. He made way too much."

They listen to her and ignore me. Figures. They fill their plates with huge portions and stand in the kitchen shoveling it into their mouths.

Kaitlyn bites back a laugh and looks to me with an expression I don't like.

"No." I shake my head.

"I'd say they already killed the mood."

"Fine," I grumble. "Have a seat, boys."

Before I know it, there are four additions to my baller date with Kaitlyn. Patrick, Jonah, Ash, and Pax groan and eat like the usual slobs they are.

"So good," Jonah wipes his mouth and then takes another big bite.

"Glad you're enjoying yourself," I say dryly.

"What's for dessert?" Pax asks as he finishes off his food and leans back. He's got spaghetti sauce on his chin and I'm not telling him. Serves him right for interrupting my date.

"I need to stop. I'm gonna be all bloated for my date later." Pat rubs his stomach, and everyone looks to him. "What? It's a valid concern. I don't work hard on this six-pack to hide it behind water weight."

"There's some pie in the fridge," Ash says. "Grab that."

I push back in my chair. "No."

They all stop and look at me.

"It's for me and Kaitlyn."

"You two are going to eat an entire pie?" Pax asks.

"Is this one of those *American Pie* movie things? Are you gonna stick your dick in the pie, Vonne?" Patrick asks, totally serious.

Massaging my forehead with a thumb, I count to three before I respond. "No. Also, gross. It's for—"

"You and Kaitlyn," they say in unison.

"But, like, all of it?" Ash asks a few seconds later.

Kaitlyn giggles, breaking the tension.

"Do you want any pie?" I ask her.

"Save me a piece for later?"

"Yeah, that's a good idea."

I cut two big pieces and then bring the pan to the guys. Dropping it down on the middle of the table, I say, "It's all yours, boys."

They attack it and I motion for Kaitlyn to follow me.

"Thanks, Vonne," they call after us.

"Sorry about that." I lead her up to my room, taking our pie and wine with us. "It was much more romantic in my head."

"Without the dick in pie references and the other guys?"

"Exactly."

I put everything on the desk and then turn to face her. She stands in the middle of my room waiting for me. I go to her and she leans up on her toes and places a kiss on my lips, lingering for a second. "Thank you."

"Welcome." I kiss her again, run my hands along her hips, gliding over that velvet fabric, and grab her butt to pull her flush against me.

Always eager when it comes to making out, she meets my enthusiasm as she slips her fingers under my shirt. I did not intend for this to go straight to sex, but damn if it isn't hard to hold back with Kaitlyn.

"Wanna play a game?"

"A naked game?" she asks, moving one hand to cup my dick through my jeans.

Groaning, I reluctantly shake my head.

"Hmmm… maybe we can compromise?" she asks.

"I'm listening."

She unbuckles my jeans and pushes them down with my boxers. My dick springs free, happy and eager.

"Fuck me first and then we can play anything you want."

The order isn't quite what I had in mind, but who am I to wreck the girl's dream date?

After we christen my desk and then the floor, we stay sprawled out there. I grab my comforter to block some of the cold from the floor and Kaitlyn settles beside me with her head on my chest.

"Are you going home for Thanksgiving break?" I ask.

"And leave you guys to fend for yourself?" She smiles. "No, I'm staying in Burlington. Holidays aren't really a big thing in my family anyway. We usually just go to a restaurant for Thanksgiving dinner."

"Yeah, I know what you mean. When I was younger, we would have these big feasts. My mom and her sisters would spend all day in the kitchen making so much food. But after my parents got divorced, we'd just do takeout or something simple and watch football. It will be weird not seeing my family on the day though."

She hums her agreement. "My dad is actually coming down next week."

"Oh, that's cool. To spend Thanksgiving with you?"

"No." She rolls her eyes. "Dalager Sports attends the career fair every year. I'm secondary, as always."

"I thought I heard someone say that he hadn't been back to the university in years."

"He hasn't. The company always sends someone to the career fair though."

I grab my wine, take a drink, and then offer it to her. "You don't think it's a coincidence that the first time he's personally coming is the first year that you're here?"

"I think it would look bad if he didn't and he knows it."

"Savage."

She's quiet and I want to press, even though I know it's a dicey topic.

"Do you really believe that?"

"I don't know. It's easier, you know? With my dad, it's better to expect nothing." She runs a finger along the rim of the glass to wipe away a drop of wine ready to drip down the side, then brings that finger to her mouth. "When I was younger, it was little things—a missed orchestra concert because he had to work late, leaving me with nannies while he went into the office on weekends, then shipping me off to boarding school because it was easier for him to not have to deal with me at all..." She takes another sip. "I haven't always made it easy on him. I'll own that, but aren't parents supposed to love you even when you screw up?"

"In theory. Probably depends on how much trouble your kids cause," I tease her.

"I was an awful teenager. I'm still pretty awful. Getting kicked out of college is among some of my finest work for sure, but there's a long list of crap that I'm not exactly proud of."

"We all fuck up."

"Not as much as I have. I push people away. I know that I do. It's just… easier."

"You don't push everyone away. I know you've dated at least the one other dude, Vivian's got your back for sure, and me."

"Vivian and I get each other. She's one of the first real friends I've ever had. And Dylan, my ex, well… as much as I'd like to put that on him, I'm the one who lit the match." Her blue eyes briefly meet mine. "I cheated on him. I know how awful that sounds. No, not just how awful it sounds—how awful it was. He was spending weekends with my roommate and lying about it, and I just needed to know how he really felt."

My heart is hammering in my chest. "So, you cheated on him?"

"I wanted to get his attention. I needed to know if he cared. So, yes, I went to the multicultural house and made out with a lacrosse player right in front of his roommate, knowing it'd get back to him." She glances at me through thick lashes and haunted eyes. "Do you hate me?"

"No, of course not." I am definitely thrown though. I never would have pegged Kaitlyn as someone who'd cheat.

"I kind of hate me for it, so I get it if you do too." Her voice breaks and she pauses, closes her eyes as if she's trying to regain composure, and then says, "I almost cheated on a test and then cheated for real on my boyfriend. Cheaters are the worst." Tears pool in her eyes and one slides down her cheek.

"Almost cheated on a test? I thought you said the reason you got kicked out of your last school was because you got caught cheating."

"A friend of a friend sent me the answer key. I didn't use it, I swear. I wanted to. I was failing philosophy. And I might as well have because the email showing he sent it to me was enough to get me kicked out."

"I'm sorry. That sucks."

"It's super embarrassing. Of course everyone assumed I had and I didn't bother correcting them."

"Why not? You shouldn't have been punished for something you didn't do."

"What's the point? Once people have a certain image of you in their mind, it's hard to convince them otherwise." She finishes off the wine and then smiles sadly as she wipes under her eyes. "If I were you, I'd probably get out now."

"Is that why you told me? To see if I'd run?"

"Maybe." Her voice is small.

I take her into my arms. "I'm not going anywhere."

Does it scare me a little that she might try to blow things up, including my heart? Definitely. But I also want to prove to her that there are people who will believe her, and who will be there no matter how hard she tries to push them away.

KAITLYN

On the day of the career fair, Lex walks me over to the event on the way to his morning classes.

"What time is your interview?" he asks as we stop outside of the building. Students are pouring inside in their suits and dress attire.

"Ten. I think I'll walk around and talk to a few other companies, try to calm my nerves."

"You're going to be great." He squeezes my hand. "Have you talked to your dad?"

"No." I shake my head. "He texted to let me know he was here and see if I wanted to grab dinner, but we have practice."

Lex nods thoughtfully. I can tell he wants to ask more, push me to open up about my dad, but he doesn't. That's one of my favorite things about him. He holds my hand and just lets me be. I know he's here if I need him, and I appreciate it, but his devotion isn't conditional.

"Do you want me to walk you in?"

"No, I think I got it from here." I palm his cheek, resting my thumb on the cleft in his chin, and give him a quick chaste kiss. "See you later, handsome."

Companies are set up around the large conference room. Folding tables covered by cloth banners take up nearly every inch of the four walls. Middle-aged men and women with big, friendly smiles stand ready to greet eager prospects.

Clutching my portfolio with my printed resume and samples for the interview, I fall into the crowd and scan the banners, looking for companies I might want to talk to. I don't really have a backup plan if I don't get the internship with Hawthorne. Vivian offered to let me crash with her at her parent's summer house in the Hamptons.

Maybe by then I won't even need a job, but I still think I want one. I've enjoyed working with the hockey team. And even though Coach Keller hired me because of my dad, I've proven to the team and myself that I am capable of doing a good job. For the first time, I feel like I have a tiny piece of the hockey world that's my own.

Dalager Sports is easy enough to spot even if my dad's dark hair and tall stature weren't familiar to me. They have a huge banner with the logo and a line of students waiting to talk and push resumes into his hand.

I approach him slowly, cutting through the line and coming up on his side. His gaze darts to me and then back to the student he's talking to. It must take a second for him to realize who he's seen, but then he looks back to me and his mouth pulls into a grin.

He continues talking and hands off his business card. The next person tries to step up, but he holds up a finger indicating he needs a minute.

I let him come to me. He wraps me in a quick hug. All I can do to reciprocate is lean into him as I continue to hold my leather portfolio against my chest. He hugs me like he's happy to see me, like he missed me, and I just soak it all in until he steps back. "I almost didn't recognize you all dressed up."

Smoothing a hand down my skirt, I say, "I have an interview."

"I remembered."

Someone bumps into me and he grabs my elbow to steady me.

"You should get back before they riot. That's quite a line."

He smiles as he scopes out the huge mass of people dying for their turn to talk to him. "Yeah, I suppose. We're still on for dinner?"

"Yeah. I'll be off work around six-thirty."

"Perfect. I'm gonna swing by the arena and see Coach Keller when I'm done here."

"You're going to the hockey practice today?"

"Just a quick stop. I'll have my phone on me and I'll meet you as soon as you're done."

Oh shit. I knew I was going to have to tell my dad where I was working, but I thought I'd be able to warm up to it and drop it casually into dinner conversation. *Oh by the way, I'm the hockey team's new equipment manager.*

Easy breezy like I haven't been avoiding all things hockey for the past eight years.

"Dad, I need to tell you something—" I start at the same time, he says, "Sorry, I need to get back."

"Yeah, of course." I take a step to the side.

"See you tonight, sweetheart."

I'm still feeling nervous and off-kilter when I get to my interview. A senior level marketing employee from Hawthorne Marketing stands from behind the conference table and offers me her hand.

"I'm Sara. Nice to meet you."

"Kaitlyn."

She motions for me to have a seat. "Is this your first interview today?"

I realize I'm still standing nervously. I sit and interlock my fingers, then squeeze. *Get it together.*

"Yes. And only."

She has the resume I emailed over in front of her. "You aren't applying for other internships?"

"No," I admit. "Working at Hawthorne is sort of my dream job."

That gets a smile from her. "Mine too. I interned when I was in college and I've been with the company ever since." She picks up my resume. "Manager for the hockey team, huh? What's that like?"

"It's great," I say with a big, trained smile. Then realize it actually is. "Smelly pads aside."

With a laugh, she leans back in her chair. "You must be a big hockey fan then."

I smile but don't provide a confirmation. Am I? My feelings for hockey are too complicated to dump on a prospective employer's lap. I know that I'm enjoying the job and being on the ice again with the team during practice has softened some of the painful memories I've clung to since I quit.

"Tell me about your experience with marketing. Any jobs or classes, projects."

I relax once I start to tell her about the classes I've taken and the ones I have planned for next semester. I take out the print copy of my Vino and Veritas marketing project and we go through that, too.

She took a few notes at the beginning of the interview, but her pen has been abandoned now as she explains the details of the internship. "I think you'd be a great candidate, Kaitlyn. Your ideas are creative and thoughtful."

"Thank you."

"Here's my card. We'll be making final decisions before winter break." She stands and I do too.

"Great, thank you for your time."

I walk out of the room and back through the fair without stopping to speak to any other companies. The cool air greets me as I push out the doors and step outside.

"Hey," a familiar voice calls out. Lex stands from a table nearby and hustles toward me. "How was it?"

"Good. I think." I let out a long breath. "What are you doing here?"

"Waiting for you. Duh." He lifts the hat on his head and runs his fingers through his thick, dark blond hair. "I, uh, heard a rumor and wanted to warn you that your dad is coming to practice."

"Not a rumor. It's true. I talked to him before my interview."

His shoulders relax. "Oh, thank god. You talked to him."

"Not exactly."

Lex's brows raise.

"I tried, but it was crazy in there."

"I don't think you're going to be able to hide it for much longer." My sweet boyfriend looks at me as if he needs confirmation that I realize I can't duck and hide for an entire practice or hope no one mentions his daughter is working for the team.

"I know. I know. I hoped I could tell him at dinner tonight, but I guess I'll have to go with the shock and awe approach." Shock, anyway.

A few hours later I'm in the equipment room fidgeting and sweating with nervous energy when my dad steps into the doorway with Coach Keller. I texted him to let him know I'd be at practice and kept it vague.

"Hey!" My voice is way too chipper and he cocks a brow. "Surprise, I'm the team's equipment manager."

He looks from me to Coach.

Coach's brow furrows, a common look, but I'm not usually the one causing it. "I'll just give you two a few minutes. You're welcome to join us on the ice if you want, Declan."

"Thanks, Coach. I appreciate it."

When it's just the two of us, he searches my face for some understanding. "Why didn't you tell me?"

"I was going to tonight."

He runs a hand along his jaw. It's been a long time since I've rendered him speechless.

"Wow. Okay." He chuckles. "My daughter is the Moo U hockey equipment manager. I did not see this coming." He grins, looking happier and prouder than I can remember from recent years."

My legs are wobbly as I take a step toward him. "Can I show you around?"

"Absolutely."

It's a strange experience walking around this place with my dad. What felt like mine, starts to feel more like his as he points out his old spot in the locker room and navigates around like he knows it as well as I do. And I guess he does.

He hangs by my side throughout practice and each time I help one of the guys he gets this big, pleased smile on his face. I have a weird mixture of feelings. Happy that we're getting along and that he's proud of me, but sad because it took eight years and hockey to put that look of pride back on his face.

I'm the last one in the locker room when practice is done. I come up short when I find the guys gathered around my dad, staring and hanging on his every word. He looks up and smiles at me.

"Excuse me, guys. Nice practice. I look forward to watching you crush Maine tomorrow." He walks toward me and I'm well aware that every pair of eyes is on us—or him, anyway.

"Hey, sweetheart."

I want to roll my eyes at the endearment he continues to use despite the fact that I haven't been sweet since middle school. "Hey. I should probably meet you at the restaurant. I'm going to be a little while."

He guides me with a hand at my lower back to the side of the room and the guys finally fall into conversation so it's not so quiet you can hear every word we say. "Look at you. I never thought I'd see you doing anything hockey-related ever again."

"Yeah, well, someone cut me off and I'm not qualified for much else."

He laughs. An easy, carefree laugh. "Listen, I'm spent. Can we do dinner tomorrow night after the game?"

"Of course," I say quickly. Am I really surprised he's flaking? I hate that I am. I shouldn't be. "I have a lot to do here anyway."

"Great. I'm going to have Coach invite the guys too. I'd like to get to know some of these kids since you're spending so much time with them. I'll call you in the morning and you can take me around, show me the campus, your dorm, whatever you want." He drops a kiss to my temple. I'm flooded with the familiar scent of his cologne and hair gel.

Before he can get out of the locker room, some of the guys thrust paper or sticks, jerseys—anything they can find, in front of him to get signed. Dad does it all with a thankful smile. He's good with his fans, always has been. I just wish those fans weren't my friends.

I busy myself with the laundry until the locker room is empty sans one hockey player that appears in the doorway freshly showered and dressed.

"What time do you think you'll be done with dinner tonight? In case a guy wanted to sneak into his girl's dorm room at an indecent hour and do indecent things." His arms wrap around my waist and he kisses my neck.

"Much sooner than you think. My dad pushed dinner to tomorrow night and is inviting the entire team."

"I'm sorry." His hard expression validates my disappointment.

"It's fine. I have a lot to finish up here anyway." I do not want his pity or even to admit that I'm hurt.

"Come out with us instead. We're going to the Biscuit for wings and beer."

"I'm not really in the mood to hear the guys go on and on about how awesome it was to meet him."

I feel him nod and then he pushes my hair away from my neck, giving him better access. He drops a tender kiss to my skin. "Okay, well, come home with me then. We'll skip dinner and I'll make you forget everything. Including your name."

"Tempting." A small smile tugs at the corners of my mouth. "I think I'm going to finish up here and then go back to the dorm and crash. I'm not really in the mood to go out. But you should go have fun with the boys. Please? For me? You deserve it. Go celebrate. You had an amazing practice tonight and I think you're really starting to mesh with the team."

He comes around in front of me, picks me up, and sets me on top of the washing machine. "I'd rather celebrate and *mesh* with you."

Then he steps between my legs and kisses me hard.

Temporarily I forget about everything but how good it feels to let him chase away the hurt. Lex is good at that. He's a reminder that someone does want me, sees my worth, thinks I'm worth blowing off the rest of the world for.

And I desperately want to believe his view of me isn't seriously misguided.

The following night, I'm prepping the locker room when Lex comes in from the ice with Paxton.

"Hey." He drops onto the bench as Pax heads toward the showers. "Are you okay? I haven't heard from you all day."

"Yes," I say, even though my hands tremble. "Sorry, in between classes, I spent the day with my dad."

"That's great."

"He's coming tonight and then we have dinner with everyone."

He wipes his forehead with a towel. "Do you want to go together? I'm a good buffer."

"I'll be okay. Thank you though."

He grins that boyish smile that makes me want to drag him into the equipment room and hide out forever. It also makes me believe that I'm capable of getting through tonight, no matter how nervous I am. One minute I want to block out the rest of the world and the next I want to conquer it. With Lex, I feel capable of both.

I'm crazy about him. I haven't told him, of course. I've been burned too many times by putting my cards on the table first. Lex isn't like anyone else I've ever dated, but if he knew how hard I'm falling for him, would he subconsciously pull away? Being the one that cares the most in a relationship is scary. You have everything to lose and none of the leverage.

"Good luck out there tonight. With Donnie hurt, you might see more playing time."

He nods. "Yeah, I know. I made Pax get here two hours early to go over some stuff. I think I'm ready." His face goes serious and I can see the nerves wash over him. "I should probably go watch some tapes or—"

"Wait," I stop him. "You got this. Have fun. Be the guy that was kicking my ass on the ice, having fun with his buddies. The twins are great together, not because they're both super talented but because they're comfortable together. They sink into a rhythm with each other, an ease that keeps their heads clear."

He nods thoughtfully. "I have so much more to prove."

"And you will." I grab him by the jersey and kiss him.

"Knowing your dad is going to be here freaks me out a little."

"Why?"

"Because he's your dad."

"Do you want me to call him? See if the great Declan Dalager has some better advice for you?"

"No," Lex says through a laugh. "I'm only interested in what the great Kaitlyn Dalager has to say. But if I have a bad game can you just tell him you're dating a frat guy or something?"

It's sort of cute, if not foolish, that Lex thinks I'd confide in my dad about my dating life at all or give his thoughts on anyone I cared about any weight.

"Hit the shower, twenty-three." I stand to get back to work. "Have *fun*."

When it's finally time to go out to the bench, I'm as nervous as the boyfriend I told to lighten up an hour ago. Way more nervous than I ever have been about this job before.

I don't have to search for my dad at all, he's sitting in VIP seats next to the bench. He's talking with the women's hockey coach, hands shoved in his suit pants, laughing—totally comfortable in his skin. Even at forty-four, he looks good and has that young, cocky way about him.

Everyone is aware of him. The players whisper and glance over at him, the crowd behind him watches. This is what it's like when my dad is in the same room—all the attention is on him. I know he doesn't purposely do anything to bring the focus to him, but I still hate it. He's dad—goofy, terrible jokes, can't cook, workaholic dad.

It's been years since he played hockey, and still, that's the only identity people see him with. If I were inclined to feel bad for him, that would be the area that I think is the saddest. The man has built an amazing company and still it's what he did twenty years ago that people want to talk about.

Lex skates by and winks at me. He makes a point not to look at my dad, and I like him even more for that.

When the puck drops, everyone finally turns their attention to the game. Including me. Lex sits on the bench holding his stick, knee bouncing, a determined set to his handsome jaw.

Donnie is out with a hamstring pull and Lex has a good chance to get more playing time. He's good enough. I know he is. Coach Keller wouldn't have recruited him, and I'd like to think I've seen enough hockey in my day to know when someone has what it takes. I'm also aware that might be the hearts in my eyes speaking. I don't think so though.

The second line comes off and Lex goes in with the third. He's so fast. Every pump of his legs is a sprint. All out. Just like he does everything. Maine is putting up a hell of a defensive effort. Lex and Hudson each get a look at the net, but both are denied by the goalie.

I'm focusing on Lex and miss how it happens but suddenly all eyes are on me.

"He needs a new stick!" Pax shouts.

I finally see Tate and his broken stick on the ice. He starts toward the bench and I grab a backup and rush forward. Tate skates by and grabs it just as Maine gets possession and sends the puck down. Tate pivots and pushes off to retrieve it before the other team can and I feel like I'm going to puke. Every second counts here.

Maine's center is breaking away and our bench holds their breath. When the ref stops play for hooking, the team lets out a relieved sigh and I finally take a breath. Adrenaline makes my heart race.

"Nice job," Coach Garfunkle says as I'm handed the broken pieces of Tate's stick. "That was close."

Way too close.

LEX

"Nice win tonight, boys," Coach Keller spits out the words as if he's afraid using a nicer tone will make the sentiment go to our heads. "Mr. Dalager has invited everyone to dinner. Be there. Use your manners."

We wait for more. He's never really finished until he undoes his tie.

His left hand goes to the knot and tugs. "That's all."

I lean back and stretch to ease some of the ache in my muscles.

"Vonne," Coach Garfunkle calls from across the room. He motions to the office and reluctantly I get up and head there, trying not to think about what Coach might want. I played quite a bit more tonight, and I think I had a couple good shifts, but Donnie will be back next weekend and I'll be bumped back to the fourth line.

"Have a seat," Coach Keller says as I walk into the office. Coach Garfunkle gives me a small smile that I can't read. Is it a pity smile bracing me for the bad news?

Coach Keller drapes his suit jacket on the back of his chair and rolls his shirt sleeves before taking a seat. Every second waiting for him to speak is excruciating.

"You played well tonight, son."

My nerves don't abate any with the compliment. "Thank you."

"I appreciate your flexibility as we've moved you around."

Two nice things in a row. Yep, the next thing is definitely bad news.

"I'm still not loving the groupings on the lines, though. You've been particularly hard for me to place. You're quick and your stick skills are as good as anyone's on the team, but that's only helpful when we can get you the puck. Scoville is a half-step behind you, and you and Thomas don't seem to be meshing like I hoped. Some of that will come with time, but my gut tells me it's not the right fit."

"Coach, I—"

He holds up his hand. I swallow hard and brace for the worst.

"Next weekend I want to try you on the second line with Hudson and Ash."

"Wait, what?" I sit forward in my chair and look between my two coaches. Coach Garfunkle's small smile has turned into a big, toothy grin.

"You and Ash have a similar style. Let's give it a go."

My mouth gapes open. I look between the coaches several times to confirm they aren't messing with me. "Thank you."

Coach Keller nods. "Show me what you got, son."

"Yes, sir."

I leave before he can change his mind.

"When Coach said we were having dinner with Declan Dalager, I thought he meant pushing some tables together at the Biscuit," Paxton says as he looks around the large back room of the nicest restaurant in Burlington. Two buffet lines are set up on either side and the servers are bustling back and forth to keep them filled.

Kaitlyn stands next to her dad. She holds a drink in one hand, the other crossed over her stomach. She's smiling but I can see the uneasiness in the way she holds her shoulders and smiles stiffly. And even from here I can tell she's giving one-word responses to the conversation.

I can't say I completely understand the issues between her and her dad, but I don't need to. A few of the guys approach Declan and I figure that's as good of an opportunity as I'm going to get to approach. She's been clear that she doesn't want Coach to know about us, but if other guys are around, then I'm less obvious. Well, if I can keep my hands to myself.

Patrick opens the circle when he spots me and claps me on the shoulder. "Nice assist tonight, Rook."

"Thanks."

Kaitlyn's dad smiles and extends a hand. "Declan."

"Lex," I say as we shake.

"Nice to meet you." He sips from the drink in his other hand.

Patrick speaks to me. "Declan was telling us about the Frozen Four game against Harvard his junior year."

I nod.

"Ah, I forget you probably don't know," Patrick says as he continues. "The semi-final game went into four overtimes before Declan made the game-winning shot."

"I was so tired I didn't even realize it went in until my teammates dogpiled me."

I'd usually be grateful for hockey talk, but Kaitlyn looks

uncomfortable and I have to think that's partly all the fawning the guys are doing over her dad.

"I guess that's where Kaitlyn got her shooting skills from," I say. Kaitlyn looks like I've betrayed her as the attention is dumped on her. Oops.

"You've been playing?" her dad asks.

"No." She shakes her head. "Just messing around a little."

I smile at her as I speak to her dad. "She nearly beat me at a shootout. Left-handed too."

"I taught her to shoot left-handed," Declan says with a proud smile that shows his teeth. "Thought it'd give her an edge."

"I'm going to get another drink," Kaitlyn says and steps away.

Fuck. I shouldn't have brought up hockey. Declan acknowledges the awkwardness with a lift of his brows and then refocuses his attention on me.

"Where are you from, Lex?"

"Phoenix."

"Arizona is a beautiful state."

"Yeah," I agree. Kaitlyn stands at the bar ordering another drink.

"Oooh," Patrick says. "They put out the desserts." He starts backing away. "Anyone want anything?"

We both shake our head and Declan and I watch as Pat makes a beeline for the dessert table.

"What are your plans after college?" he asks me. "Are you already signed?"

A nervous chuckle escapes. "No, sir."

"Did you play juniors?"

I shake my head. "I got a late start. I didn't touch a hockey stick until I was sixteen."

"Seriously?"

A knot of frustration builds in my chest. Which is absolutely ridiculous. I can't seriously blame myself for not discovering how much I loved hockey until I was a teenager.

"It wasn't a sport anyone I knew played. There were club teams, but I did all the usual sports my friends did. Football, baseball, basketball, track."

Still, I fight the feeling of annoyance that I'm continually paying for those first oblivious fifteen years of my life.

"Well, I'd never be able to tell. You're a natural."

"Thank you." A prick of warmth on the back of my neck. "I feel like I'm constantly playing catch-up with these guys."

"I'll let you in on a secret." His smile reminds me of Kaitlyn's. They have the same shape mouth, I decide. "That feeling never goes away."

"You started late?"

"Eleven. Not as late as you, but I understand the push you're feeling to prove yourself and make up for lost time."

"Wow." The word slips from my lips. "I didn't know. Kaitlyn never said."

He studies me as he takes another drink. "Are you and my daughter close?"

Oh shit. If there's a right answer, I can't find it in the seconds that Declan Dalager stares me down, waiting for one. Paxton and Tate have joined her at the bar. She looks everywhere but at us.

"I like to think I know her pretty well."

"Is she happy?"

Fuck. This guy throws punch after punch at me, and I am not prepared. He's either a really good actor or he cares more than Kaitlyn thinks he does. Maybe it's guilt that makes him ask. I don't pretend to think he's some great guy just because he was an amazing hockey player. He hurt my girl—intentional or not and that makes me distrustful of him.

"I don't know, sir."

He nods and gives me an apologetic smile as if he realizes it's a tough ask to speak to anyone else's mindset. Especially Kaitlyn's.

"You don't have to worry about her, though. She's resilient and tough, and just... amazing. And if she needs it, we've got her back. She's one of us now." If he doesn't already know that, he should. And with that, it's definitely time for me to walk away.

I bow out just as Coach Keller steps up to talk to Declan and I do what I should have done a few minutes ago. I check on my girl because the team might have her back if she needs it, but I want to be there even when she doesn't.

I nod to Pax and Tate. Kaitlyn is turned toward the bar. I take her hand and tug. She smiles hesitantly.

"Let's go home, baby doll."

Kaitlyn's dad stays through the next week. We don't have any classes after Tuesday, but the extra time is spent practicing and preparing for our games this weekend. And in the in between time, Kaitlyn is either working or with her dad. The rest of the guys might be glad the amazing Declan Dalager is in town, but I kind of wish the guy would go away. Selfish, I know, but I miss having her to myself.

Wednesday he drops by practice and I can tell it makes Kaitlyn less confident. The verdict is still out on whether or not I think he's a decent person. Maybe he's unaware of the difference in his daughter when he's around, or maybe he doesn't care. I haven't figured it out.

Other than that, practice is going well, though. Coach was right—Ash and I are good together, and I'm feeling more comfortable on a line with him and Hudson than I have any other combination. Maybe all this switching will have been worth it.

Thursday, after a long, grueling practice, we load up for the three-hour drive to Amherst. We'll get in, have a dinner out to celebrate and then hit the hotel for an early night. I'm excited about the game, but more pressing at the current moment is that I get to finally spend some time with my girl.

She scoots over to make room for me, and I take the seat next to her. She's looking out the front of the bus and then the windows as if she's looking for something.

"Did you forget something?" I ask.

"No. My dad is coming. He's following the bus."

"He's going to the game?"

She nods, still feverishly looking for him.

"Wow. Does that mean things are going well between you two?" I've tried not to ask, hoping she'll confide in me if needed, but I'm dying to know how she's feeling.

"Yes. No. Maybe." She sighs and slumps down in the seat and abandons her search. "I can't tell if he's interested in spending time with me because I'm his daughter or because it's something hockey-related."

"You two have done other stuff since he's been here. It hasn't all been hockey."

"True. I just wish I'd have found a job doing something else so that I'd know it's me he truly cares about."

"Is that why you quit hockey when you were a kid?"

She searches my face.

"What? I know you didn't really quit because you suddenly stopped enjoying it. I saw the look on your face when we had the shootout. It's the same one I see during a game when we score or when you get called on to make a quick adjustment or change. You love it. Even if you wished you hated it."

"At first, hockey was something we did—just the two of us. But as I got older, it became another place that I felt inferior. And, yeah, I loved it when it was this special and sacred thing, but not when I realized people were watching me so closely. I was under a magnifying glass all the time when I was on the ice. And coaches were terrified to give me any type of instruction. They probably thought my dad would blow a gasket or something if they gave me the wrong advice."

"Gotta admit. That doesn't sound so awful to me." I give her a rueful smile. "I nearly got laughed out of the place when I showed up to try out for my local club team and they found out I'd never played before, save some goofing off and camps the summer before."

"You worked hard. I think that's really admirable." She leans her head on my shoulder. "Anyway, it was easier to let him have that world and find things of my own. I just didn't realize it was the only thing holding us together."

"Maybe, let it be a bridge. Something you both love that helps you connect and then work on the rest."

"A bridge?"

"Yeah." I kiss the top of her head. "You gotta start somewhere."

"Vonne," Coach Keller barks my name and I jump. I'm not ashamed to say the man scares me on the regular, but I'm sweating bullets as I realize I just kissed Kaitlyn in front of him.

"Yeah, Coach?" I ask and then clear my suddenly squeaky voice. Kaitlyn moves her head from my shoulder.

"Back of the bus, son. You two can canoodle on your own time." He moves to his seat.

"Well," I say, looking at my girl. "Looks like he knows."

"Kill me now," Kaitlyn groans. "Canoodle?"

I chuckle at her embarrassment and then kiss her. At this point, what difference does it make? Reluctantly, I stand. "Later, baby doll."

KAITLYN

Dad's waiting for me in the hotel lobby when the bus arrives. Since the team's in Amherst to play, my dad rented a car and came with us. He'll drive the rest of the way back to Boston tomorrow after the game. *One more day.*

I drop my stuff in my room and we walk over to the restaurant next door ahead of the team.

"I forgot to ask how your interview with Hawthorne went?"

"Good, I think. I won't know anything for a while."

"I still have a contact over there, I could–"

"Oh my gosh, no." My face heats with embarrassment at even the idea of him calling to put in a good word or ask a favor. "Dad, that's horrifying."

He chuckles. "Okay, okay."

"Promise me that you will not pull strings to get me a job. I want to do this on my own."

He smiles, a proud type of smile that I haven't seen in a long time. "I promise."

"Speaking of internships," I say. "Did you extend any offers yet?" Dalager Sports summer internships are extremely competitive. Even people that don't care about hockey (though, let's be honest, those people are few and far between) line up for the opportunity to work there. The office is in a great location downtown Boston, the pay is the best you could hope for, and NHL players are known to wander the halls. Two summers ago, a kid got scouted and signed thanks to a pickup game with my dad and some of his friends.

"Not yet, but I have a good feeling I'm just about to find the perfect person."

"Did any of the guys from the team apply?" We wait for the team in the front area of the restaurant.

"A few did, yeah."

The guys start to catch up to us. They're eager to eat, and probably to hang with my dad some more. I don't think I'll ever get used to people fawning over him.

The past week with my dad, things have been… good. It feels more comfortable between us than it has in a long time. I'm not going to lie; I think part of the reason this visit has been different is because of the boy walking toward us.

Lex grins. Hands shoved in his pockets, he ambles slower than the rest of the guys. He always seems to know just what to say or do to help me focus on the here and now instead of obsessing about the past.

Let's be real, I haven't made it easy on my dad. I've made a lot of bad choices. When things get hard, when I feel out of control, I lash out in destructive ways. So even though I'm still carrying a lot of resentment and anger, I'm trying to enjoy the time with him.

And I don't think I realized how much I missed chatting hockey with him. Am I worried it's the only reason he's proud of me now? Sure. But I'm trying to give him the benefit of the doubt. If that's our common ground, our bridge as Lex called it, then I suppose it's as good a bridge as any.

I grab Lex's hand as we're led to a long table in the back room of the restaurant.

"Hey," I say. "Dad, you remember Lex?"

I drop my boyfriend's hand so he can shake with my dad.

"Of course, good to see you again." My dad's smile is big and genuine as his gaze darts between us.

"You too, sir," Lex says.

Before we can take our seats, my dad says, "Excuse me. I'll be right back. I'm going to get a drink from the bar."

Once we're seated, Lex places a big palm on my thigh. "If I didn't know better, I'd think I'm your buffer."

"Or maybe I just wanted to have dinner with my handsome boyfriend."

He huffs a laugh.

"Okay, yes, a little bit of a buffer. Things are better, but I still feel like I'm walking on eggshells with him."

Like I'm going to blink, and his disappointment will return.

"Well, I think I can suffer through. I'll just avoid any mention of hockey, Boston, New York, your childhood…" Lex glances up like he's trying to think of more taboo topics.

I swat at him playfully.

He leans in and kisses me softly. "I'll be your buffer, baby doll. Any time."

"Ugh, you two. It isn't fair that Vonne gets to bring his girlfriend to games." Patrick tosses a straw wrapper at us. The twins and Tate are on the other side of Lex, and the rest of the team and coaches fill out three big tables pushed together.

"Better watch yourself," Lex says, hand still on my leg. "My *girlfriend* is in charge of the smelly goodness."

I roll my eyes. I swear, of all the things I do for this team, it's still the laundry that they're most concerned with me sabotaging.

Patrick's face goes slack with shock. "You can't change up a guy's routine like that mid-season, Dalager. That could have major repercussions."

"The laundry detergent has major repercussion?" I bite back a smile.

"Well, it isn't hurting it," he grumbles.

Lex chuckles next to me. "We're serious about our routine."

"Yes, I see that. I promise not to sabotage game day laundry," I announce to a relieved group of ridiculous jocks.

Dad returns and the servers start to hustle back and forth from the kitchen, bringing out drinks and taking food orders. The mood stays light throughout the meal, and I start to relax more with every passing minute. Lex is a good buffer. He doesn't suck up to my dad, but he chats and helps keep the conversation away from all the banned topics.

Coach Keller stands at the end of his table and someone calls out, "Speech!"

The head coach shakes his head, but there's a smile on his face as he begins to speak. "Enjoy your meal and then get some rest. Curfew is ten, same as always. We've got a tough couple of games this weekend and you all need to keep your heads on straight."

Someone down the table makes an inappropriate joke and Lex snorts and then as if realizing my dad is across the table from him, straightens. I love how likable he wants to be.

"Do you think he'll notice if I make a roommate switch?" Lex whispers where only I can hear.

"Maybe."

"Probably still worth it."

"Worth not playing tomorrow?" Coach Keller takes absolutely zero shit from his players. He will not hesitate to bench anyone that shows up late or breaks one of his rules.

He grimaces. "Damn, it's a real tough call. I think your boobs edge out victorious though."

I smile and laugh and absolutely don't believe him. "You are going to be great tomorrow."

I say the last part loud enough that my dad overhears.

"Lex, Kaitlyn said Coach switched up the lines for tomorrow."

"That's right." Lex can't hide his grin.

"She also tells me you've been working hard, even outside of practice, to earn more playing time each game. That's great." My face warms a little. I didn't realize how much I told my dad about Lex.

He squeezes my thigh under the table. "Yeah, it's trippy, but I'm excited."

"What are your plans for the summer?" my dad asks as he leans back in his chair, beer in hand.

"Going back to Arizona, most likely. I'm covering my own room and board so I have to work as much as I can in the off-season to save up."

I didn't know that, but it doesn't surprise me. There are only so many hockey scholarships. Even insanely talented players like Lex don't always get full-rides.

My dad nods speculatively. "What kind of work?"

"Probably working for my dad. He owns a tire shop."

"And what about hockey?"

"Oh, I'll still practice every day and I'll get on the ice with some of my old teammates as much as I can."

Of course, he's already planned out his summer training regimen. His dedication is something I admire about him. I've never loved anything that much. At least not in a long time.

"You know, Lex, Dalager has internships over the summer. We always hire first from Burlington before looking at other applicants."

I feel a prick of annoyance at the underlying tone like

working at a tire shop is somehow not as good. I'm not sure that's how he means it, but it certainly comes off that way.

Lex doesn't seem offended. "Yeah, I think Kaitlyn mentioned that. It's awesome that you still look out for your alma mater."

Dad nods. "I've been going through the applicants this week, and I noticed you didn't apply."

"Oh, well…" Lex looks to me for help, but I can't find words fast enough. "Working in an office isn't really for me."

His grip on my leg tightens.

"I get that." Dad chuckles lightly. "A lot of the jobs are your typical office grunt work, but we have one opening in particular in our testing department that I think might interest you. If you give me your application, I can put it at the top of the stack. A summer of testing sticks, skates, pads… it's a pretty cool job."

He's basically saying the job is his, but I can't tell if Lex realizes that or not. My boyfriend looks shell-shocked and doesn't respond.

Dad keeps right on selling it. "You'd be close enough to still commute back to Burlington on weekends to train or—"

"Dad!" I find my voice.

They both look at me, but I avoid meeting Lex's gaze.

"He has a job," I say. "He doesn't need your handout."

"I didn't mean it like that," he says at the same time Lex says, "Kait, it's okay." He faces my dad. "I really appreciate the offer."

"But?" my dad asks with a smirk like he can't believe Lex might turn him down.

"Can I have a few days to think about it?"

"Absolutely."

I pull my leg away from his grip under the table. Lex shoots me an apologetic grimace of a smile. My head is going to explode and now I'm angry at both of them and I can't figure out why. Why shouldn't Lex want a job working in a field he loves and where he can be close to school? It would be a great opportunity for him, and I'd get to see him more. Girlfriends want good things for their boyfriends, right? Then why do I suddenly feel like I want to cry?

"I think I'm going to head back to the hotel. It's getting late." I stand abruptly.

"I'll come with you." Lex starts to get out of his chair, but I stop him.

"No, it's okay. Stay. I'll be fine and I really would like to be alone. I suddenly have a throbbing headache."

I know Lex well enough to know he'll follow me no matter what I say, but I get a stroke of good luck when Coach Garfunkle stands to give the guys more instructions for where to meet and what time tomorrow morning. I should probably hear the instructions as well, but nothing is more important than fleeing this second.

My room is the first place Lex will look when he finally does come after me, so I hide out at the hotel bar. It's large and I find perfect cover beside two big guys that block me from the doorway.

I take two shots of tequila before my brain starts working, deciphering what just happened and picking it apart. My frustration at my dad turns to frustration at Lex. He knows how sensitive I am about my dad and people using me to get to him. He just sat there and acted like everything was fine. He needs a few days to think about it? My stomach knots at the thought of it. Would he really work for my dad?

The liquor makes my face warm and feeds my anger. I don't know if it's justified, but I know it's how I feel. Why don't I want Lex to work there? Have I really held such a grudge that him working there feels like betrayal or is it something else?

And is it too much to ask of my dad to like me more than my hockey boyfriend? He's met Lex twice and he's just offering up amazing opportunities like they grow on trees. Or maybe he really is just trying to help him because he's my boyfriend?

Ugh. I don't know and I hate that I don't because I should. If nothing else, I should know without a doubt that my father loves me more than hockey or his company. Because if he can't love me like that what chance is there anyone else can?

I manage to avoid Lex all night, but his calls and the frequent knocks on my door throughout the night keep me from sleeping well. I'm not sure what it says about me that I don't want to give him a chance to explain his side. I guess it feels like opening myself up to pain. Inviting it in and letting it take what's left of my trust and hope.

I hadn't realized how much of that Lex holds in his hands.

Somewhere after three shots of tequila, I very sanely decided that I would talk to Lex, but first I needed to figure out how I feel about him taking the job and what it means for us. Because of course he will. I texted him to say we'd talk tomorrow and that he should go to bed and rest up for the game. He listened.

I sleep through my alarm. I must have shut it off in that hazy place between conscious and unconscious. The room phone is what finally wakes me. I reach for it and bring it to my ear and mumble some unintelligible greeting.

"Kaitlyn? This is Coach Garfunkle. We're all downstairs waiting on you. Everything okay?"

I fling myself out of bed with the phone still at my ear. "Yes. Yes. I'm so sorry. I'll be right down."

I'm at the bus three minutes later. I don't meet anyone's eyes, but I feel all of theirs on me as I take my seat up front. Last night's alcohol sits uneasy in my stomach and even after brushing my teeth, my mouth feels dry and gross.

When we get to the arena, I throw myself into the job. I grab the heaviest bag and take off toward the door with superhuman strength. At least for a few steps.

"I got it." Lex tries to take it from me, grabbing the handle.

I hold tight. "I've already got it. Thanks."

I don't look at him. I can't. The only way I'm going to get through this game is to not look at his face. Of course, my stubborn boyfriend doesn't give up right away, so I mumble, "Seriously, I'm fine. Please." The last is a plea that goes way beyond needing him to let go of the bag.

"Okay," he says. His tone is sad and resigned, and he takes off ahead of me.

20

LEX

This should be the most exciting game I've played all season, but my head isn't in it. Kaitlyn won't look me in the eye. I know it isn't the time or place, but I just need two minutes with her to figure out what the fuck happened last night.

One minute I was acting as her buffer, sweating my ass off, trying to talk to her dad and hopefully take some of the heat off her, and the next thing I know he's offering me a job. A great job. That is not even in the top one thousand ways I would have predicted last night going.

Coach is at a loss for words after the first period. Turns out, he's even scarier when he's quiet. I should be dissecting my abysmal performance, but I know why I suck. I slept like crap and I'm distracted.

At the first opportunity, I try again to talk to Kaitlyn.

"Hey, uh, can you change the lace on my right skate?" It's a bogus request, but it does the trick. She nods and I take a seat in a free chair next to her.

We have just a few minutes before the second period starts and zero privacy, but I need something.

"Are you okay?" I whisper.

"Fine." She doesn't even look me in the eye. Though to be fair, I asked her to change my lace, and that's what she's focusing on.

"Kait." I grab her wrist. She freezes, but still stares down. "I don't understand why you're freezing me out. Talk to me."

She moves her hand and finishes the job. "How's that feel?"

"Skate feels fine, but I feel like shit. Please, tell me what you're thinking?"

"Vonne," Coach Keller says only my name, but the request is clear. *Stop focusing on your girlfriend and get out there.*

I can't budge though. She's hurting and I want to help.

"I'd never work for your dad without talking to you about it first. I didn't know what to say. He kind of put me on the spot."

Those beautiful blue eyes finally land on me, but they hold no warmth. "It's a great opportunity. Did he give you his card? He did, right? You're as good as in. You'll probably meet a lot of really important people in the hockey world too. You'd be an idiot to turn it down." She stands and moves to the back of the bench, picking up a few water bottles that were tossed to the ground.

"I don't care about that." I move in front of her so that she has to face me and grab her hand. I need to touch her. Kaitlyn needs touch. She reacts to bold gestures and unrelenting determination. Not because she's high maintenance, but because she's been disappointed too many times. Polite doesn't cut it with her.

"You should care. You're a great hockey player, but connections are everything."

"And I appreciate that he offered, but I can do this on my own." The buzzer sounds. "Can we talk after the game? Let me take you to dinner when we get back to Burlington."

"Sure. We'll see."

"Kait—"

"Roddy," Coach Keller barks. "Take Vonne's spot on the second line since he can't be bothered to warm up with the rest of the team."

Fuck.

I know I deserve it, even should have expected it, but my stomach drops and I feel like I might throw up. My chance. I finally got my chance and I just blew it.

There's a flash of concern in Kaitlyn's eyes as she says, "Please go. We both have people counting on us right now. We'll talk later."

I don't see any playing time for the rest of the game. We lose by one after a strong third period by Mass. Ask me if I care. No, that's not even true. I care. I really, really do. Later I know I'll be punching myself, but I can't see past my need to talk to Kaitlyn. It was a misunderstanding. I froze, and yeah, maybe there was a few seconds where I wondered what it might be like to take the job.

Paxton corners me in the locker room. "What the hell, man?"

"Not now, Pax." I'm already half-undressed so I can get the hell out of here and catch her before the bus ride back.

He puts a hand on my shoulder to keep me from moving. "What was that today? You get an opportunity that you've been working for and you just blow it?"

"It was a long night. Kaitlyn—"

"Nah, I don't care why. You busted your ass for today. *I* busted my ass. Late nights, weekends… Nothing else should have mattered. You let yourself down, but you let the team down, too."

No one else talks to me, and that's probably for the best. Pax's disappointment speaks volumes. And he's right. He put in a lot of extra time to help me out. The weight of my screwup is starting to sink in. I may not get another chance to prove myself.

Coach Garfunkle silently shakes his head as I try to take the seat next to Kaitlyn on the bus. I slide into a seat halfway back and shove on my headphones. Then spend the entire ride back to Burlington stewing in self-pity.

I should have turned Declan down as soon as he offered. I was so shocked, and I didn't want to be rude. And then there's that small voice in my head that says maybe I didn't because some part of me wanted to say yes.

Coach Keller waits until we've arrived in Burlington and are filing off the bus to stop me. "Hang back a minute, Vonne."

Kaitlyn glances at me, but then goes with the rest of the team. I slump in a seat across from Coach. He's discarded his jacket and tie. He looks older sitting sideways. His big frame takes up most of the space between seats. Resting his clasped hands in his lap, he starts in with a much nicer tone than I was expecting. "Do you know why we wanted you at Burlington?"

"Because of my high school stats?" I ask dumbly. It seems pretty obvious to me. I was offered spots on a lot of teams all across the country.

"Impressive as they were, you didn't have the experience we usually look for."

My heart sinks a little. I know it's a statement of fact, but damn, it always feels like I'm having to apologize for it.

"You have something else. Something I admire even more than skill," Coach says, and I hang on his every word. "You have tremendous heart. Your determination and love for playing on this team is a coach's dream. I can't give guys talent. I show up each day and make decisions that I hope benefits each of you individually, but ultimately, I have to do what's best for everyone. It isn't a job I take lightly. If I cut a guy, I know what it's costing him."

He pauses to let his words sink in.

Shit, am I getting cut?

"You are a talented kid, Lex. You don't need me to tell you that. You wouldn't be here if I didn't think you had what it takes, but it was your work ethic and determination that brought you here. And if you want to be a contributing member of this team, that's what it'll take. Nothing less."

"I do... want to be a contributing member, I mean."

"What you do on your free time is your business, but when it affects your performance, you make it mine. I don't want to see you and Kaitlyn within ten feet of each other at practice or games unless it's about equipment. And I don't want to hear about you two hanging out at the hotel or anywhere else while we're traveling. She's doing a great job for us, but if you pull another stunt like today, it'll cost both of you."

I swallow the lump in my throat and nod.

"Understood?"

"Yes sir."

I find the guys at the Biscuit. There's already a stack of empty shot glasses on the middle of the table.

I take a seat next to Pax. "I'm sorry for today. I do appreciate how much you guys have helped me and I won't let you down again."

"Forget about it. We've all had off days." Pax slides a glass in front of me and gestures to the pitcher of beer.

If only it were this easy to fix things with Kaitlyn.

We order more wings and shots and keep the conversation away from hockey. For once, I'm happy not to bring it up. I have no interest in reliving today.

I take Coach's words to heart and don't call or go see Kaitlyn. Maybe a night to clear our heads is the best thing for both of us.

Tomorrow I'll do better. On all fronts.

21

KAITLYN

On Saturday, I get to the rink early. I left a load of laundry in the washing machine last night and I still need to do one more load before the game today. I haven't heard from Lex except a text this morning that said he wanted to talk after the game.

Through the grapevine, I found out that Coach threatened to bench him again today if he didn't get his head straight. That was enough to keep me from reaching out last night even after I'd calmed down and decided I should hear him out.

I feel awful. AWFUL. I know better than anyone what this means to Lex. Maybe we're more alike than I thought because yesterday was a classic Kaitlyn move in blowing up your own life.

I might be confused on how I feel about him working for my dad, but I know that I want Lex to succeed at something he's worked so hard for.

When everyone arrives and the team starts getting ready, Lex and I manage a few quick glances. He stays focused on hockey and I treat him like any other player.

After last night's loss, there's a different air in the locker room. Serious and focused and ready for redemption in front of their home crowd.

As the team takes the ice for warm-ups, I help Kirk on the sidelines. His pads have become the headache that never ends.

"I'm going to order a different brand of leg pads for you to try. And let's remeasure too and see if we can get a better fit."

He nods. "Dad's still here, huh?"

"What?"

He points with a gloved hand to the section next to the bench. Sure enough, there's my dad. I wave awkwardly.

Kirk chuckles. "You didn't know?"

I avoid answering that outright and instead say, "I'm sure he just wanted another chance to see the team play."

"You might not have known, but Lex did. I saw the two of them outside looking chummy before the game. Heard he offered him a job, too."

My voice wavers. "When did you see them together?"

"Today. An hour ago. Well, hey, if he's handing out free jobs to anyone you're fucking, mind if I tell him we've hooked up?"

I push his leg off my lap. "You wish."

He shrugs. "Can't blame me for trying. Kind of impressive, really. There's no way he was getting any attention from your dad without you. Is the sex with Pretty Boy really that awesome that you're okay with being used like that? Now *I* could show you a good time." He smiles and leans in closer.

I hold my breath. He's vile—inside and out. I know this, but his words still sting.

"Shouldn't you be in the net?" Paxton asks as he skates up. His jaw is set, and he glowers at Kirk.

Kirk hesitates, glancing between Pax and me before he takes a step back. He pulls his mask down over his face, but I can tell he's still got that slimy smile aimed at me. "Offer's good anytime."

"Are you okay?" Pax asks.

"Fine." My tone says the opposite, but Pax just nods.

"He's a jerk. Whatever he said, brush it off."

Easier said than done.

The loss last night was effective in getting the guys back focused and it's like we're playing against middle schoolers. They stand no chance. Lex has a great game, too, and I can tell it's a weight off his shoulders to prove himself.

Dad texted to see if he could take me to dinner after the game. No mention of why he made another trip to Burlington. I've seen the man more in the past week than in the entire last year. I'm trying really hard not to be bitter about how much hockey has played a part in those visits.

Lex is waiting for me when I exit the arena. He pushes off the side of the building, his bag slung over his shoulder. "Hey."

"Hey."

"I'm sorry I couldn't talk to you earlier. Coach was pissed about yesterday. He put the fear of God in me."

"It's okay. I get it. Nice game tonight."

"Thanks." He smiles and takes my hand. My pulse quickens and my stomach dips. "I'm also sorry about the other night. I didn't know what to say or do when your dad offered me the job."

"You could have said no."

Lex winces. "I froze. Turning him down immediately seemed rude. It was a nice offer and I'd make way more than working the tire shop. It felt like the least I could do was be appreciative and hear him out."

"And did you hear him out?" My body tingles all over with

frustration. Not just at Lex, but at myself. This is everything I hate about being Declan Dalager's daughter.

"Yeah." Lex nods slowly. "I called him this morning."

"*You're* why he came back?" I drop his hand and cross my arms over my chest.

"No. He came here to see you."

I laugh, dry and bitter, sucking the cold air into my lungs.

"Let's go to dinner and talk to him. I think if you hear him out—"

"I cannot believe this. After everything I told you. You know how I've been used in the past and still you take the first opportunity he thrusts in your lap. How quickly you jumped to taking his side. I don't want to hear him out. Things were perfectly fine before I started pretending that we had anything in common outside of hockey. We'll never see eye to eye and I just need to accept that. If you want to take the job, take the job, but I'm not going to stand here and listen to you try to play it off like you're doing me a favor by getting in the middle of it."

He strokes my cheek. "No, that's not what this is. I want things to be better between you two, yes, but I called him and asked him to come back because—"

"God, you really had me fooled. All of your talk of hard work and doing it on your own." I pull away from him. "You invited him here, you go to dinner with him."

"Kait," Lex calls after me. "Kaitlyn."

"What do you mean, you quit?" Vivian sits on the edge of my bed and looks at me like I'm a crazy person. I feel like one.

"I called Coach as soon as I got back to my room. I don't want any part of the team or hockey..." Or Lex. My heart is broken. Even through my anger, I can feel those jagged pieces of my heart wishing things were different.

"Are you sure he did it maliciously? Lex doesn't strike me as someone who would use you to get ahead."

"Malicious or not, he knows that taking a job with my dad would hurt me. He knows and he's going to do it anyway."

"Maybe he—"

"Can you just be on my side on this one?" I ask. "Please. I really need someone in my corner."

She smiles sadly. "Of course. Always. Do you want to order food? We could stay in and watch ugly cry movies."

"Let's go out tonight," I suggest. I need a distraction. "Girls' night. Just me and you like the old days."

"Okay." She seems surprised by the request.

"God, I can't believe this. Why couldn't I have fallen for a nice boy that hates sports? I'm an idiot."

"Listen closely because I'm only going to say this once. You know how I hate to get all mushy. You are amazing. You're all tough on the outside, but inside you're a big old softie. Like real deep down." She grins.

I fall back onto my bed. God, I'm pathetic.

Vivian is quiet and I stare up at the ceiling, thinking of Lex and all those times we spent together, him adamantly denying he wanted anything to do with my dad. Was it all a lie?

"Put this on." A dress lands on my stomach.

I sit up with the black, silky material in my hands. "I don't feel like dressing up."

"Exactly," she says and brings a pair of shoes to me too. "When you feel like crap, you should look like you don't. Fake it `til you make it."

What I feel like doing is curling up into a ball and crying. That or drowning my sorrows in several shots of Kahlua... while wearing sweats.

"Chop-chop. We leave in fifteen minutes."

I'm bombarded with people wanting to chat and catch up as soon as Vivian and I walk into the multicultural house. After a month of hanging out pretty much exclusively with the hockey team, my stock has gone up.

None of these people are really my friends, but I spent enough time hanging out here that it's a bit like a homecoming.

Vivian pushes a cup into my hand, and we go to the basement. On one side of the room, old couches are pushed against the wall and a wooden table is being used for cider pong. The other half of the room is where a few people are dancing under a disco ball. My best friend pulls me in front of a large speaker. Music with a heavy bass blasts into the basement, making it hard to hear my own thoughts.

Vivian dances and I sort of sway back and forth. In order to dance, you have to be able to feel something. I'm numb.

I get Vivian's attention and motion to the other side of the room. She nods and I leave her to dance. She'll be there most of the night.

I'm deciding between cider pong or depressingly standing alone like some kind of wallflower, when I spot Emmett at the pong table.

"Kaitlyn?" He's holding a pong ball and the rest of the table looks to him expectantly. He tosses it without really looking and walks to me. He crushes me in a drunken hug and then slides his hands down my arms. "Look at you. I've missed you."

He wraps me in another hug. Emmett was never this touchy before. We made out, yes, but leading up to the kissing he was more aloof. Then, I'd liked that he played hard to get. It made the kissing that much more exciting. I thought it meant he'd be worth it, but instead it only meant he really wasn't that interested.

"Hey, Emmett," I say and step back, putting some distance between us. "Looks like you're having a good night."

His green eyes are droopy, and he grins. "The best now that you're here. I've missed seeing you around. I tried to text."

"No, you didn't."

"Well, I didn't have your number, but I wanted to."

I don't roll my eyes, but I really want to. "I'm not that hard to find."

He doesn't offer up an excuse, just smiles drunkenly at me. "Come play pong. You can be on my team."

I hesitate, and he tips his head toward the table. "Come on. It'll be fun."

I follow with absolutely zero enthusiasm. The only good thing about playing cider pong is that I'll be drunk in thirty minutes and care a lot less about everything.

The cups are refilled, and Emmett and I stand on one side of the table across from two of his lacrosse buddies.

"I'm surprised to see you here tonight," Emmett says. "Heard you've been hanging at the hockey house."

I hum a response. One of the guys on the other team drops a pong ball into one of my cups. The cider is room temperature and bitter. It makes me think of the delicious cider I had at Vino and Veritas. And of course, that makes me think of Lex.

Emmett drops an arm around my shoulders. Casual but claiming and just… wrong. Lifting his hand, I remove it and step away. "I've gotta go. Thanks for the game."

"But we aren't finished," Emmett says.

"I am."

I turn and my gaze goes immediately to Lex across the

room. My heart squeezes because he's here, but then his expression twists into something hard and unforgiving. He starts walking toward me. Ash and Vivian are a step behind him.

We meet in the middle. "What are you doing here?"

"I had a feeling you'd be here." Hurt flashes in his eyes. "Don't worry," he says flatly. "I'm not staying long. I just needed to tell you that I turned down the job. This morning when I called your dad, I thanked him for the opportunity, but I told him no."

"But he came to Burlington. Kirk said you two were talking before the game."

"He came for you. I called him, but only to turn down the job and to tell him that I thought you two should talk. I know it isn't my business, but I wanted to help. He can't fix it if he doesn't know how you feel."

My mouth opens and closes but no words come out.

"Kaitlyn." Emmett appears at my side. He nods his head to Lex and then looks back to me. "You coming back to play, babe?"

Wishing the floor would swallow me up, I say, "No, Emmett. I'm good. Thanks for the game."

"Cool. I'll catch you later on tonight before I leave."

I let out a shaky breath when Emmett finally walks off.

"So." Lex looks around. "This was your way of breaking up with me, huh?"

"I just needed a night out with Vivian."

"But this is your usual place to cheat on boyfriends, yeah?"

That stings, but I guess I deserve it. I didn't come here to hook up with someone else, but I understand why he might not believe me. Still, it's another blow to realize that's really what he thinks of me.

"Listen, if that was your plan, to cheat on me so you'd have an out, well consider it done. No need to hook up with one of these slimeballs to do the job. Just tell me it's over."

"Is that what you want?" I ask and close my eyes to brace for the answer.

"Nah, uh-uh. I've been nothing but honest about what I wanted from the beginning. You aren't turning this around now. What do you want, Kaitlyn?"

A simple question with no easy answer. So I don't give him one.

His blond head hangs. "Okay then."

He turns to leave.

"Wait," I call.

He pauses, but I don't know what to say to make him stay. Or even if I should.

"Bye, Kaitlyn."

22

LEX

"Hey, we're going to the rink. You coming?" Tate asks when I get downstairs Sunday morning.

"Nah."

"Cool, I'll meet you over there." He pauses at the back door. "Wait, did you just say no?"

"Sure did. Have fun." I leave him staring at my back while I walk away. First things first, I need to go back upstairs and put on sweatpants because it's cold as fuck in the house. Then, I have big plans of making enough breakfast for four, eating it all myself, and parking my ass in front of the TV.

I've done two out of the three when Pax calls.

"Yo," I answer, clicking on the TV.

"Where are you?" my buddy asks with worry in his tone.

"Just chilling at home. Seriously, chilling because it's fucking freezing outside." I laugh at my own joke.

"Well get over to the rink. We're doing edge work drills, your favorite."

"No thanks. I'm good." I tap end and get busy flipping through the channels.

I don't spend a lot of time in front of the TV. For one, it requires sitting still and then there's that little voice in the back of my head always telling me that someone else out there is working harder.

The guys give me shit for not having an off button, but that little voice has made all the difference. Today, though, I've temporarily shut it up with carbs. I haven't had a pity party in a long time. I'm due. Plus, there's so much cool shit to watch.

I'm on my sixth consecutive episode of some weird exotic animal zoo reality show when the back door creaks open. Ash, Jonah, and the twins file into the living room and take a seat.

"Have you guys seen this shit? It's wild," I say with a slight head nod of a greeting.

"Uhh, yeah, we watched it like right after it released," Ash says.

"I thought the whole world did. You never watched it?" Jonah asks.

"Uh-uh." I wave a hand toward the kitchen. "I made chili and cornbread if anyone wants some."

"Ooooh yes," Ash says, and they all hurry to the kitchen.

A minute later, Patrick calls, "Uh, Lex?"

"Yeah?"

"There isn't anything left, rookie."

They march back into the living room carrying the empty cornbread tin.

"Oh, right." I pat my stomach. "It was good, sorry. There's some cheesecake in there, though. Maggie brought it over."

"You mean this cheesecake?" Pax flips open the top of the box and tips it so I can see the mangled sliver of cake left.

I shrug.

"O-kay." Ash stands in front of the TV. "I think it's intervention time."

"Fuck off. I'm fine. You guys take days off all the time."

"You don't though," Pax points out.

I sit up. "Yeah, well, maybe I should have. Hockey isn't everything, right?"

"Oh shit, he's gone real dark. It's worse than I thought." Ash's eyes go wide with concern.

"I'm fine," I grumble and head out of the room away from their pity. My stomach gurgles in protest as I take the stairs. Admittedly, I may have eaten too much.

I lay in my bed and close my eyes. My sheets still faintly smell of Kaitlyn. She hasn't called. Neither have I, to be fair. I can't keep chasing after someone who doesn't want to be caught. I know she's slow to trust, but at some point, I have to accept that it's never going to be enough. She has to want to trust me, and I don't think she does.

All my life I thought hard work was the answer to everything. I was wrong. No matter how hard I try with Kaitlyn, I'm never going to earn her trust. What if effort only makes up a small percentage of luck? I'll have spent my entire life busting my ass trying to have things I'll never get.

Monday, I call in sick. I don't really call anyone. I email my professors to let them know I won't be in class and then I walk downtown. Burlington is a cool city. There are so many quirky, fun places—many I've never been in.

I decide to take the day and see them all. Maybe I have been too focused on hockey and pushing myself.

I walk by the maple store, which smells heavenly, but my stomach is still queasy from taking down an entire cheesecake yesterday. The pizza place isn't open yet and I avoid the Biscuit in case any of the guys come by for lunch.

I'm about to turn around and go home, maybe binge another TV show, when I see the sign for Vino and Veritas. I hang a right and go into the bookstore. Among the shelves of books, people of all ages peruse the spines. I'm looking for nothing in particular, but also feeling like I'm looking for something, too.

I get to the magazine section and automatically go for the first sports one I see, then grab the one next to it instead. Taking it to the one empty chair, I flip through the pages of a woodworking magazine. Then I trade it out for one on fishing. Maybe I could be into fishing. Can you make that a career?

A little girl toddles in front of me. She puts her little hand on my leg, drool sits in a pool on her bottom lip.

"Uhh, hi," I say and glance around for her owner. She must have walked away from her parents. "Where's your mommy?"

She grins and the drool from her lip drips down onto my leg.

I sit up and do another sweep of the place to locate someone who's missing a child. She crawls up into the chair with me and I have little chance to do anything but scoot over and make room for her.

"Book!" Her chubby hand points to the magazine in my hand. She sits upright waiting patiently like she expects me to read it to her.

"Oh, no, I'm not… this isn't…"

"Book!"

I wriggle from my seat and put the magazine back. I have a shadow now. She follows me. I try to stop her, but she squeals with delight as if we're playing some game of cat and mouse.

I locate one of the employees but she's assisting another customer. This kid is just straight-up lost because no one is looking for her, and now I'm a little freaked-out.

I'm not paying attention to her, instead frantically checking up and down each section of books for her parents, when she pulls a book down off a shelf. She falls under the weight of the book and starts to cry. Now people are looking at me in that way they do when they're shaming parents for not keeping their kid quiet.

"She's not mine," I assure them. No one cares.

I scoop her up and try to console her.

"Daddy!" she wails and points to the far side of the room.

"Your daddy's over there?" I ask and point to the wine bar.

She just keeps pointing and crying, so I walk her over to the bar and hope I'm not committing kidnapping.

The bartender, Rainn, looks up from the bar as I enter with the wailing toddler.

"Tommy, your daughter picked up another one," he calls.

"Does she belong here?" I ask, holding her out.

A guy walks out from the back and the kid wriggles until I put her down.

"Lily!" he says as she runs and hugs his calves. "You can't run off, sweetheart."

He picks her up and kisses her cheek. "Thank you," he says, cradling her sweetly and then carrying her off toward the back. "Drink's on me, buddy."

I slump onto a barstool. "Holy crap."

"You all right there, my man?" Rainn asks. "You're pale and kind of sweaty."

"I thought I was going to have to call the police or take her home with me like a stray puppy."

Rainn puts a glass in front of me. "I don't think it works like that with kids." He wipes down bottles while I drain the non-alcoholic cider. He remembered my drink, or it was a guess. I get my answer when he asks, "Where's your girlfriend today?"

I'm not even sure she is my girlfriend anymore. "Classes probably."

"Uh-oh. I know that look. What happened?"

"That might work when you're serving alcohol, but I'm not opening up over this non-alcoholic shit."

He snorts. "Fair enough. How about an order of maple pigs?"

"Slow day?"

"I've got about another hour to kill before it picks up. Humor me?"

"Maple pigs and a cheeseburger. And another cider. And something sweet for dessert." My stomach cramps as if it knows I'm about to torture it again.

"That's forty bucks for an hour's worth of entertainment," he complains. "This better be one hell of a story." He goes into the back to put in my order and I pull out my phone.

I've got texts from Ash and Pax wondering where I was for our usual morning workout and another from Jonah asking why I wasn't in our English lit class. Still nothing from Kaitlyn. I need to stop expecting to hear from her and accept that isn't the way she operates.

When Rainn returns with a basket of maple pigs, I start talking. I'm sure it's mostly nonsense, but he listens while I ramble. I finish the maple pigs and then he sets a cheeseburger in front of me and I devour that too.

"I didn't realize you were a hockey player," Rainn says when I finish. He's got that same look of disgust on his face that Vivian always wears when the subject comes up.

"Not you too. I've never met so many people that hate hockey. Isn't it sacrilegious here or something?"

"Probably. So, you were pissed at her for getting you in trouble with the coach and then killing your opportunity with one of the coolest jobs ever?"

"No." I shake my head. "It was my fault I got benched and I knew just the thought of working for her dad would hurt her."

He hangs his head and snores. "Get to the good stuff. Where's the drama?"

"She assumed the worst and wouldn't hear me out. She pushes everyone away and I guess I thought I was different. I don't know what to do."

"Only two options."

"And those are?" I ask.

"Let her push you away or don't." He shrugs.

A couple of guys walk into the bar and take seats at one of the tables.

"Looks like my hour is up," I say.

He checks his watch. "Yep. You better get to practice. Coach Keller will eat you alive if you show up late. You're already on thin ice, don't make it worse."

"How do you know Coach Keller is such a hard-ass?"

He avoids eye contact as he clears my plates. "Everyone knows that."

I don't have time to press him because he's right, if I don't hurry, I'm going to be late.

"Thanks, man. I appreciate the food."

"Yeah, well, next time I'm holding out until I hear your story. That was barely worth it. Good luck." He winks at me and heads toward the table with two beers.

I jog back to campus. Two days of eating like I'm on death row was not a great idea. I don't really feel like practicing, but I can't let the guys down again. I might be willing to sabotage myself, but not at the expense of the team.

I'm wheezing by the time I make it to the locker room. I collapse onto the bench, holding my side.

"Are you all right?" Tate asks, giving me a slow once-over.

"Too much food," I gasp.

"Better get a move on. Coach is in a particularly foul mood."

"Why?"

The man himself walks in before Tate can answer. Hands on his hips, he doesn't meet anyone's gaze as he barks out, "Let's go, boys. Vonne, are you planning on practicing in street clothes?"

"No, sir."

"I'm gonna need the freshman to take care of the equipment today. Daniels and Forte, get us setup. Since Vonne's not ready, he can do the cleanup."

"What happened to Kaitlyn?" Jonah asks.

The entire locker room looks to me for an answer. I drop my gaze to the floor. My stomach rumbles and there's a deep ache that has nothing to do with the amount of food I ate. I do not have a good feeling about the answer to that question.

"Our equipment manager quit. We'll get another one, but for the next few days, everyone needs to pitch in." He straightens. "Now, let's get moving. We've got BU this weekend and they would love to give us our second loss of the season."

I know I should be getting dressed, but I can't move for several minutes after Coach leaves.

"You didn't know, I take it?" Tate asks.

All I can do is shake my head.

"Too bad. I'm gonna miss the way she laced my skates."

"There goes my good smelling jersey," Patrick says, holding the fabric up to his nose and inhaling. "Way to screw it up for us, Rookie."

I'm still staring at the ground when Paxton starts handing me gear. "Get dressed. With Coach's mood, there's no telling what he'll make you do if you're late getting out there."

"Thanks." I start removing clothes and putting on whatever Pax hands me. I'm in a daze, not really seeing or feeling anything.

"Which skates?" he asks.

"What?" I look up at the two pairs of skates in my stall. My old skates, the ones I thought Kaitlyn had thrown away are tucked nicely next to the new skates. They've got fresh laces and they look as good as you could expect a pair of overused skates to look.

She hadn't thrown them away at all. She held on to them. Not just held on to them, fixed them up the best she could in case I decided to use them again.

"Lex?" Pax says my name.

I snap out of it and reach for the newer skates. "I got it. Go ahead. I'll be there in a minute."

"All right." He takes a step to the door. "But hurry."

When I'm dressed, I take one last look at the old skates on my way out the door. She held onto them. I don't know what it means, but it has to mean something.

KAITLYN

Listening to Chastity have sex with Dylan is awful, but the sounds coming from her room right now are even worse.

They're laughing. I can't make out their words, but I can tell he's teasing her and she's responding with lighthearted sass. Then more laughing.

I lay on my bed and listen. I don't even try to drown them out. I'm a glutton for punishment. Am I ever going to have that with someone again?

Their laughter stops and a few minutes later Chastity's door opens and shuts. I pull myself upright and let out a sigh. It's practice time and I hate that I'm not at the rink. And I really hate that I hate it.

Two months ago, I would have laughed in my face. Sad about missing hockey practice? Sad about no longer having a job? Ha! Yet here I am wishing things were different and wondering how long it'll be until I stop hurting. Moving on has never been a problem for me before, but I've never let myself get this invested.

I trudge into the bathroom. Maybe a shower and a fresh

face of makeup will help. When you feel like crap, look like you don't, as Vivian says.

Chastity is in our shared bathroom. The smile on her face falls when she sees me.

"I didn't realize you were here," I say.

"Same. You're not usually here in the afternoons anymore."

"Well, I am now," I snap and then feel like an asshole. "Are you going to be long? I want to shower."

"Five minutes."

The Chastity I met at the beginning of the school year would have given me the bathroom and scampered off scared. Dylan's been good for her self-esteem.

I start out of the bathroom and then pause. "Take your time. I'm not in a hurry."

A confused expression crosses her face. I'm never polite to Chastity. She stole my boyfriend. Even if I no longer want him, I can't forget the way they went behind my back. I think a peace treaty is in order, though. We have an entire semester left and I don't want to feel like an asshole every time I run into her in the bathroom.

She looks around. "Is everything okay?"

"No." I laugh. "Nothing is okay, but we have to live together. I'm sorry I've been such a bitch. Can you two keep it down when you're screwing though? It's a real killjoy."

Her cheeks pink immediately. "Yeah, of course. You'll do the same?"

There's that backbone again. I hardly think that'll be necessary now that Lex and I broke up, but I nod. "Truce."

While I'm waiting for Chastity to finish in the bathroom, there's a knock at my door. I open it quickly, surprised when it's my dad on the other side.

"Hey. I didn't realize you were still in town."

"You would if you ever answered your phone." He motions with his head down the hall. "Let's get some dinner."

Since I have nowhere else to go, I follow without argument. Neither of us speaks on the way to the restaurant. Once we place our orders and drinks are placed in front of us, he leans forward. "What's going on with you? I thought things were better with us and then Lex called and said I should come back so we could work things out."

"I was upset that you offered my boyfriend a job. And that he seriously considered taking it."

"Why?"

"Please don't ask me to psychoanalyze myself. It's scary enough living in my head without having to make sense of it."

That gets a light chuckle from my dad, but his smile is sad.

"I hate that I never know what's sincere and what isn't with you. Second-guessing every move you make is exhausting."

"I'm sorry if I overstepped. Lex seems like a bright young man and I've never seen you so taken with anyone. I just wanted to help."

"When have you ever seen me with anyone?"

"I've seen enough to know you're different with him."

"I'm not debating that I am, but seriously, how would you know? You shipped me off to school when I was thirteen and I've never brought anyone home."

"I may not have been there every day, but I can tell quite enough over the phone and by your actions."

"I knew you'd like Lex," I admit.

"And you still dated him. I'm shocked."

Yeah, me too.

"He doesn't need you to give him a job, you know? It's a great opportunity and it might make it easier for him if he has connections, but he's going to make it to the NHL all on his own. He's incredible. I've never met anyone more determined and focused."

"It wasn't a pity offer, Kait. You seemed to care about the boy, and I wanted to make things easier for him. Lex is a talented hockey player. He has some work to do on handling his emotions, but he'll learn the same way we all do. No one has infinitely good days."

"How did you do it?" My dad hasn't had an easy life. Especially those early years when he was still playing hockey. His marriage ended, he became a single father, and then he lost his mom.

"It was easier for me because I had you to worry about. Any time I felt like giving in to a shitty day, I'd remember that someone else was depending on me."

I play with my straw wrapper while I give that some thought. When I try to look at his decisions over the years through that lens, I can almost forgive him for not loving me enough to keep me near him.

"I assume Lex told you he turned the job offer down?" Dad asks.

"He did. I'm sure he was trying to spare my feelings, but he should at least consider it. We broke up anyway so there's no reason he should decline."

"He also recommended that I offer you the job."

"What?" I give him my full attention for the first time tonight. "Me? But…" My words trail off.

"He seems to think that you don't hate hockey as much as you pretended to all these years, and he says you're a hell of an equipment manager."

"Of course, I don't hate hockey. I quit when I was a kid because I was mad at you. I felt like the only time you really cared about me was when I was playing. I ruined it to see what would happen. And I was right. You shipped me off to boarding school that next year."

"Those two things weren't related. After you quit hockey, you also started lying to me about where you were going to be and then sneaking out when I said no. I knew you were acting out, but I didn't know how to stop it. I never cared about you quitting hockey, Kaitlyn. Well, that isn't entirely true. I cared because it was the one place I could connect with you."

"Then why did you send me away?"

He runs a hand along his jaw. "I really just didn't know what else to do. I wanted the best for you even if that meant I wasn't it. I was just a year older than you are now when you were born, and I didn't know the first thing about being a dad. Your mom wasn't dependable, and it was all on me. I thought I had it under control until you became a teenager and then it was super obvious that I was in way over my head. When you started getting into trouble, I didn't have a clue how to handle it. You'd already been through so much and I was scared I was failing you too."

I'm silent, processing and a little overwhelmed if I'm honest. We've never openly discussed my mom leaving. She was a part of my life. She called and sent cards. She even breezed into town and surprised me on occasion. But I always came second to the men in her life. She flitted in and out of my life like the seasons and I accepted it like it was normal. For some reason, I'd always found her abandonment easier to forgive. Maybe because we'd never been close. My dad and I had been, though, once upon a time.

"I know that I wasn't an easy kid to love, but I just wanted to know that you'd be there no matter what terrible thing I did." I interlock my fingers and squeeze to relieve some of the anxiousness I feel admitting that I want my father to love me. I've spent my entire adult life adamantly denying it.

"I loved you even when you were getting into trouble. I'm sorry I didn't do a better job of showing it."

Since I've already admitted more than I planned to tonight, I continue, "Do you know that my whole life people have used me to get to you? Even in middle school boys started to piece together that spending time with me meant more face time with you. Every time I meet someone, I worry that once they find out who my father is, that's the only identity they'll associate with me. Staying away from hockey made that easier. I was so leery of Lex in the beginning, but he made me believe that he genuinely liked me for me. You blurred the lines by offering him a job. If he takes it, I'll never know if he's with me because of the opportunities available to him or because he likes *me*. And if he doesn't take it then I'll feel guilty for standing in his way."

"There will always be reasons not to trust Lex or the next person that comes along. For what it's worth, I don't think Lex thinks of you as a way to get to me. Actually, I think it's quite the opposite—he wants to use me and a job offer to spend more time with you." My dad smiles.

"He doesn't need your job, I stand by that, but I do think it would be dumb of him to turn it down. Let me talk to him again before you hire someone else."

"Okay, I will keep the spot open for him in case he changes his mind. And one for you. I built Dalager for us. No expectations or pressure." He raises his hands defensively. "But my life's work was to ensure your future. I had little to fall back on after I quit playing professionally. I had a degree that no one cared about, and I didn't want to be one of those guys trying to milk sponsorships for the rest of my life."

"I don't know what to say." Tonight has been a lot. I haven't seriously considered working at Dalager since I was a kid.

"You don't have to say anything. If you want to intern or have a job after college, then it's yours." He regards me seriously. "Assuming you keep your grades up."

"The marketing needs work. Linda is a dinosaur," I say, speaking of his current head of marketing.

He full body laughs, and it breaks something between us. "She was the best there was fifteen years ago, but admittedly she isn't a big fan of change."

"If I take an internship, does that mean I'm taking Lex's spot or anyone else's?"

He smiles and studies me. The weight of his gaze is heavy and penetrating. "No, sweetheart. You won't be bumping anyone else's opportunity."

"Thank you."

"While we're being honest, I think you should reconsider quitting the team. From what Coach Keller tells me, and from what Lex says, the guys speak highly of you."

I can't imagine Coach Keller saying that, but it's nice to hear anyway. "Thank you, but I think it's for the best. They'll get someone else quickly."

"Just think about it. I better understand your reasons for giving it up, and I wish I'd known years ago why you quit playing, but don't let other people ruin something you love. Not even me. And I will stay out of the way with Lex and the team. I promise not to interfere or put you in a weird spot."

"Thank you."

He nods. "Though I would like to visit more often."

"I'd like that too. How do you feel about watching basketball?"

He makes a face. "For you, I guess I'll suffer."

24

LEX

I'm half asleep on the couch when the door to the equipment room swings open. She stands in the doorway unraveling the purple scarf around her neck.

"I was waiting on the washing machine," I say as I sit up and run a hand through my hair. "What are you doing here?" Her unexpected arrival makes me feel hopeful for all of two seconds until I read the apologetic look on her face.

"I, uh..." She trails off, voice small.

"I heard you quit." My voice is still rough with sleep and my tone snaps conveying every bit of anger I'm feeling.

"Coach Garfunkle said it would be a few days until you guys got another equipment manager." The guilt on her face and the way she avoids eye contact says everything she won't.

"You don't need to quit, Kait," I say and stand, moving toward her. I lift my hand to touch her and then think better of it.

She notices. Walking past me, Kaitlyn peels off her coat and drapes it, along with her scarf, on the back of a chair. "It's for the best."

"For who?"

She finally meets my gaze. Her blue eyes shine with pain. "Everyone."

"You can't really believe that. I know how much you loved working for the team. Even when you didn't want to."

"I cost the team their perfect record and I interfered with what should have been your big opportunity to step up. I could never forgive myself if I ruined things for you. I know how hard you've worked and what it means to you. There could have been serious repercussions for the drama I caused. So, yes, I absolutely believe it's best that you have an equipment manager that can do the job without adding any personal drama. My quitting makes it less complicated for you."

"I don't care." Exasperated and annoyed, I clench my hands. She's martyring herself. It's so twisted and so completely in character that I can't believe I didn't expect it.

"You do. I know that you do. You're right, I have loved being the team's manager. Hockey is a part of me I thought I'd lost. I have that back, largely thanks to you. I am so grateful, but I also know that there are other people better suited for the job. Let's be honest, I got the job because I'm Declan Dalager's daughter."

My stomach drops. I hate that she always thinks she's second best to her dad. "Maybe that's how you got the job, but you're good at it. You *are* the best person for the job."

I can tell in the set of her shoulders that nothing I say is going to change her mind. She's so goddamn stubborn.

"Anyway, I'm glad you're here," she says softly. "I wanted to apologize for Saturday. I was mad, but I didn't hook up with Emmett." Her gaze drops to the floor. "I won't blame you if you can't believe me when I say nothing happened. I deserve that."

It strikes me in her tone that she isn't about to fight for me.

She's saying goodbye. Even though I walked away Saturday night, I guess I still hoped she was going to realize she wanted to be with me regardless of all the bullshit.

"I could never hurt you intentionally. Not even to protect myself. I realized earlier that might be how you feel too. I know you wouldn't take the job at Dalager if it would hurt me."

"Never."

"And that's why you should take the job. After everything you've done for me, I don't want to stand in the way of anything that makes getting what you want easier. I mean it. I talked to my dad tonight and made sure the offer was still good. It'd be a great opportunity and you should definitely take it. Please don't let the things I said hold you back. You can save for next year's rent while staying close to school and still working out with the team."

She still doesn't get it. Time and again I've tried to show her that she's more important and she just refuses to believe it or simply can't. Yeah, before I met Kaitlyn, hockey was my entire life. She changed that. She changed me. "I don't care about the job. God, you're so exasperating. When are you going to get it through your head? I want you. The rest is bullshit."

"Lex—"

"No, I'm done trying to prove myself to you. I'm done believing that if I just try a little harder, I can make you see how crazy I am about you. At some point, I've done everything I can and it's on you. You have to fight back for what you want. Whatever that is. Decide what's worth it and what isn't but stop running away and pretending you don't care what happens. Take some goddamn responsibility."

I fling the door open before she can say a word and march out of the locker room. The walk back to the house in the cold does absolutely nothing to cool my temper. I slam the back door shut behind me.

"Welcome home, sunshine," Ash says from the dining room table with an amused smirk.

I blow out a breath as I pace. I'm shaking.

"Everything okay?"

"I yelled at her," I say and wipe my palms on my thighs. "Holy shit, I actually yelled at her."

Ash chuckles. "Good."

"Good? In what world is that good?" I growl. "She makes me insane."

"You've been more than patient with her. No one can fault you for not trying."

"I'm done. I give up. Nothing I do will be good enough."

"Do you know how to give up?"

"I hate that she's always waiting for the other shoe to drop, for people to disappoint her. And I hate it even more that that's exactly what people have done to her all her life. She thinks everyone is going to let her down because past experiences pretty much guarantee it."

"And you don't want to be another person that proves she's right?"

I shake my head. "I don't think there's anything I can do to make her believe me."

"So, walk away. You'll have a clear conscience that you did everything you could and there are plenty of girls out there that would be a lot less hassle. Do you wanna go out tonight?"

I groan and elicit another chuckle out of him.

"Give it up, Vonne. You and I both know you're not really ready to give up. But for tonight, I'll play along." He grabs two beers from the fridge. "I'm texting a few of the guys. Let's get stupid."

I down one beer and am working on the second when

Jonah walks in the back door. "I brought tequila and a case of beer. What are we feeling?" He lifts both hands.

Ash ushers him forward. "Both."

The back door opens again and Tate steps inside. "Hey, sorry. It was hard to pry myself away from Maggie."

"Not helping right now," Ash says.

"Sorry." Tate takes one of the beers. "How are you doing, buddy?"

"Swell." I unscrew the cap of the tequila and toss some back straight out of the bottle. I immediately regret that.

Tate takes the bottle and sips in solidarity. I love these guys. No questions asked, no fucking games. They've always got my back.

"It's really over with you and Kaitlyn?" he asks.

"Definitely." My chest aches with the finality of it. I won't go after her. Not again.

"I can't believe she quit. I thought for sure she'd change her mind and show up at practice."

"She did. I ran into her while I was waiting for the laundry."

"Did you convince her to come back?" Jonah asks.

It doesn't escape me that the guys want her back as much as I do. I wasn't blowing smoke up her ass, she really is good at being our manager.

"Genius here yelled at her." Ash points his beer in my direction. "I doubt we'll be seeing her around anytime soon."

"Real smooth," Jonah says with a chuckle.

The bottle makes its way back to me and I take another healthy drink. The back door slams again. I glance up to see who else is here to witness the drunken spiral I'm about to go down.

"What the hell, Lex?" Kaitlyn storms in and stomps her way in front of me. The cold radiates around her, but she is fire. Eyes blazing, cheeks red from the freezing temperature outside.

The guys go completely still except their heads which volley between me and Kaitlyn with rapt interest.

"Uhh…" I stand.

"I was trying to pour my heart out to you, and you ran off before I could tell you that I want you too. I was trying to fight for you." Her arms are flailing, and I've never seen her so fierce about anything. She's a beautiful force of nature. "That's why I made sure you still had a job and why I'm still doing the laundry for the team. For you, you big dummy." She shoves at my chest. "I screwed up and I'm sorry. I should have believed you, but I was scared."

It goes quiet. My teammates are staring at me with open, gaping mouths, waiting to see what I'm going to say or do. They're easy to ignore as I study Kaitlyn's face for sincerity. "Earlier that was you fighting for me? That timid, soft-spoken girl?"

"I was getting there!" She tosses her hands up again and looks to the ceiling. "I needed you to know how sorry I was first. Because, I am, so sorry. You deserve every opportunity that comes your way, no matter who puts them in front of you." She kind of screams the apology, but it still warms something in my chest.

A half crazed and half delirious snicker escapes from my lips. "Wow. I totally misread you. I thought you were saying goodbye. You're not used to groveling, are you?" I lean in with a playful smirk. "Pro tip, usually when someone's fighting for you, you realize it."

Like now.

Jonah drops his head to the table. "If this guy can get a girl, anyone can."

"I could wait and put it on a billboard, or you could just

say you accept my apology and kiss me." She's still basically yelling, but I'll take it. This girl, the one yelling and stomping through my house, she's the girl I fell in love with.

"Really?" Hard work for the win. Or maybe it's just love conquering all. I'm going to choose to continue to believe that love is like everything else – it works only as hard as you do. And I'm a damn hard worker. That's never going to change.

"Really."

"Say it again."

Her eyelashes flutter closed, and her chest rises and falls with a deep breath. "I'm sorry, Lex. Truly."

I shake my head. "No, the other thing about wanting me."

Her mouth pulls into a smile. With an eye roll, she does. "I want you, you big idiot. Kiss me before I come to my senses."

So I do. I hold back nothing. I kiss her like my lips might be the magic touch to erase all her past pain. A balm and a promise. I can't change what she's been through, but I can show her every day how much I want her. Now, today, tomorrow. If she's willing to fight, so am I.

KAITLYN

"What can I get you?" the girl behind the counter at The Green Bean asks when Lex and I step up to order.

"Oh, umm..." I peruse the menu like I don't have the thing memorized.

"I'll take a small coffee," Lex says while I continue to deliberate.

"I'll try the vanilla iced latte. Small."

"I got it." Lex pulls out his wallet and hands over his card to the cashier.

"Thank you. As soon as I get another job, I'll repay you."

"Not necessary. My mom got a bonus at work and sent me some cash for essentials."

"Buying your girlfriend coffee isn't essential."

"Agree to disagree." He kisses me and we move down to get our drinks.

Vivian is here studying for a test and we take seats across from her.

"What'd you get this time?" she asks as I take a sip.

"Vanilla latte. Not bad. This might be it."

"Finally found your drink?"

"I think so." I lean my head on Lex's shoulder and he wraps an arm around my waist.

"You two are killing my vibe here."

"Sorry, not sorry," I say and kiss him on the cheek.

"Hey, man." Someone claps Lex on the shoulder, and we all turn. "Good luck at tomorrow's game. BU's looking good this year."

"Yeah." Lex chuckles and swivels in his seat to give the guy his attention.

I turn back to Vivian. "My boyfriend is more popular than me."

"Don't worry, honey, you're prettier." She kisses the air.

It's actually pretty sweet to see people fawning over my boyfriend.

"Speaking of the game, do you want to come with me tomorrow night?"

"Oh no," she says and sighs. "I feel very conflicted between morals and obligation."

"No obligation necessary, but it should be a good game."

She hums. "It was so much nicer when you were working for the team and I could just meet up with you after. Yes, of course I will be there with you. What colors are BU?"

"You can't wear rival colors, Viv. We'll be flocked and tossed out."

Lex turns back around. "Did I just hear Vivian agree to come to our game tomorrow night?"

"She did. Just look for the dot of red in the student section."

"That'll go over well."

Vivian shuts her laptop and stows it in her backpack. "Okay, I gotta go to class. Wish me luck."

"You've got this," I tell her. "Text me later."

Lex stretches out and drapes his arm around the back of

my chair. "Are you sure you're okay coming to the game tomorrow?"

"Of course. I wouldn't miss it. Why wouldn't I come?"

"Okay. It's just that I know it might be hard watching the game from the stands instead of the bench. I wouldn't blame you if you said you'd rather get the highlight version from me after, is all."

"I still want the highlight version." I lean forward and place a kiss on his lips. "But I will absolutely be there. I finally get to cheer for my boyfriend like a normal girlfriend."

He grins.

"Well, assuming Viv doesn't get us kicked out."

Ash appears at the end of the table with his backpack over one shoulder and a scone in hand. "Hey, Vonne, I've been trying to get a hold of you all morning." He slides into the seat Vivian vacated.

"I left my phone at the house," Lex says. "What's up?"

"I talked to my uncle and we're on for this summer. Six weeks of parking golf carts and wiping down clubs, and we can stay in his house rent free. We just have to cover utilities."

"No way." My boyfriend's mouth pulls into a big smile. "Really?"

"Really. You in?"

"Yes. That's amazing. Thank you."

"Awesome." Ash takes a big bite of his scone and smiles around it. "I have to run or I'm going to be late. We'll talk details later."

"What was that about?" I ask.

"His uncle owns a golf course outside of Boston. You're looking at the newest cart boy."

"What about the internship at Dalager?"

"I called your dad again this morning and told him I couldn't take it. I appreciate that he held it open for me, and yeah, maybe it'd open some doors for me, and it'd be fun as hell, but I need to do this on my own."

"I can understand that."

"But, I can still stay close to school and even closer to you."

"I haven't heard back from Hawthorne yet. They said they'd contact everyone before break."

"You'll get it. I'm sure of it. Things are looking up for us."

"You're cute when you're optimistic. And congratulations, I'm really excited for you. What's your dad going to say about you not going back to Phoenix this summer?"

"I think he's expecting it. Last time I talked to him, he told me he'd hired another part-time high school kid." Lex finishes his coffee. "Ready?"

"I don't want to go to class. I'd rather hang out with you."

"I'll come by tonight after practice."

I nod even as my heart squeezes, thinking about another day of pacing my room during practice. I really need to get a freaking hobby or something.

Lex walks me to my building, kisses me hard, and heads down the sidewalk to his own class. I slip into my seat in the middle row as the professor writes on the whiteboard.

The girl next to me is staring and I give her a small smile. We've sat next to each other all semester, but we've never spoken.

"Hi," I say. "I'm Kaitlyn."

Her smile gets bigger. "I thought so. You're—"

I brace for it and coach myself not to flip out on her. There's no escaping my father. *She's just curious, don't make her feel like an ass for asking.*

"Lex Vonne's girlfriend," she finishes.

It takes me a second to realize what she's said. When it hits, I smile back. "Yes. Yes, I am."

"I'm Naomi." She leans on her elbow. "You are a legend. I

heard that the first time you met Lex, you tossed a beer on him." Her eyes are big with admiration.

I decide I like Naomi and I prepare to tell her the whole story. "Actually, it was my friend Vivian who poured the beer on him."

Friday afternoon I head over to the arena before the game against BU. I assumed they'd have no trouble finding another manager, but it looks like tonight they'll be on their own. I give Coach Garfunkle a quick rundown of how I've reorganized things in hopes it'll all go smoothly tonight.

"I'm sorry," I say for the second time.

Coach Garfunkle waves me off. "It's all right. We've managed without before, but are you sure this is what you want?" His gaze narrows.

I wonder if he's checking out my aura and if he can see right through the lie I tell when I say, "Yes, I'm sure. And you guys are managing fine without me."

"That's because we have a laundry fairy."

"A laundry fairy?" I bite back a smile.

"Mhmm. Someone has been coming in at night and doing the laundry. Any ideas?"

"I just didn't want to leave you guys in a bad spot like when Alec left."

"And we appreciate it. Truly."

"I'm surprised you haven't found anyone yet. There must be lots of people dying for the job."

He nods. "Yeah, there are. Takes a special person though. Our equipment manager has to fit with the team as well as any other position."

I smile. My chest aches and I want to cry. "Thank you for

everything. I will prep the locker room tonight. It's the least I can do."

"We'll miss you around here."

"Oh, here." I take the crystal he gave me from the desk and try to hand it to him.

"You keep it." He backs out of the room. "Good luck, Kaitlyn. If you ever need anything, I'm here."

I blow out a long breath and drop into the chair, clutching the crystal in my palm. I'm deciding between going ahead and crying or forcing myself to get up and get busy when there's a knock on the door. Paxton steps in and lifts the elbow pad in his hand. "Hey, Kaitlyn. Sorry to bug you. Do we have an extra one of these?"

"Uh, yeah." I shove the crystal in my pocket, grab a backup pad, and we swap. He lingers awkwardly. "Anything else?"

He takes a step back. "Nope. All set. It's good to see you."

No sooner than he's gone, the other Graham brother appears. "Yo, Kait."

"Hey, Patrick. Need something?"

"Do you have…" His eyes scan the room like he's looking for something. "Cups?"

"Cups?" I turn to the stack of them on the wall. Usually, the guys come in and grab them as needed. It's the one piece of equipment they don't usually ask me to fetch. "Sure. Take what you need."

He hesitates, but then grabs one and salutes me with it on the way out. "Miss you around here."

Weird.

But not as weird as Jonah entering after he's gone. He looks uncomfortable and nervous. My confused glare probably isn't helping. "Can I help you?"

He's holding his skates and lifts them. "Could you sharpen these?"

"Now?"

"Yeah. If you have time. I like how you always fix the laces and spray them before you return them."

Amused, I take them. "Sure, I'll do it before I leave."

Which would happen faster if he left the room, but he stands there staring at me.

"It'll be a little while," I say, in case he's waiting for me. "I'll leave them in your stall."

"Okay, yeah. Thanks. I really appreciate it. You're a good manager. We miss you."

When Jonah gives me his back, I stand there to see who's next. Are they afraid they're going to be without a manager forever?

Tate fills the doorway and I wave him to the side. He sidesteps so I can get by him and sure enough, there's a line of guys waiting for their turn.

"What is this?"

I glance at a shy freshman whose gaze darts to the ground. Ash smirks but doesn't speak.

"Anyone want to fill me in?" I ask. "Or should we just continue whatever madness is going on here?"

"It's our way of asking you to stay." Lex steps out from the end of the line. His long legs eat the space between us. "We're a team. That includes you. We need you, Dalager."

"I don't know what to say." My heart races.

"Say you'll stay. Fight with us. BU is going to be tough. We need all our best players."

"That includes you," someone says.

"Thank you, guys, but you won't be without a manager forever. You'll find someone and they'll be so excited to work with you. They'll be nicer, too."

Coach Keller pushes into the locker room. He's holding a stack of papers. "Twenty new resumes and they're all terrible.

Dalager, thank goodness you're here. What do I have to say to get you to stay? Want me to make these knuckleheads clean up after themselves more?" He smiles. A real honest to goodness smile. He shakes the papers at Lex. "That one's in love with you, so I think I could get him to do just about anything you want. Laundry, spraying pads… you name it and I'll put him in charge of it."

Lex's mouth falls open.

"I don't think that'll be necessary." I look from Coach to Lex to the rest of the guys. "You're sure?"

"We're sure," they say in unison.

Lex holds up a green jersey and turns it so I can see the back where my last name has been ironed on, then tosses it at me. "You're never getting rid of us now."

"Guess not. Did you do all this?"

"Nah. The guys were as anxious to have you back as I was. And Coach Keller, that was coincidence."

I put on the jersey over my shirt. It might be silly, but it really does make me feel like a part of the team.

"How do I look?"

"Beautiful." He grins and then puts his hands in his pockets. "I should get dressed."

"Yeah, okay." My heart is hammering in my chest. I can't believe he did this for me. He's always showing up for me. Big, ridiculous gestures.

"Wait." I grab his elbow and pull him closer. I hesitate. "I want to kiss you, but I don't want to get fired or get you benched."

"Yo, Coach," Lex yells without taking his eyes off me. "Is it okay if I kiss my girl?"

"Make it quick," he says in an annoyed tone. "The rest of you stop gawking and get dressed."

Lex steps forward and slowly brings his lips to mine. This

feeling is like nothing else I've ever felt. If I think of the past as leading me here, it's a little easier to accept that I blew up so many good things to get to this better one.

He pulls back and rests his forehead against mine. "Coach kind of stole my glory earlier, but he's right. I love you. Like a ridiculous amount. Maybe enough to spray the pads every day."

"That is ridiculous, but I might hold you to it. And I love you too."

"Ticktock, Vonne," Coach Keller yells.

Lex chuckles. "I gotta go."

"See you out there, twenty-three."

My phone vibrates in my pocket and I wince. Shit, Vivian's out there waiting for me. I go out to greet her. The stands are packed as usual.

"Look at you," Vivian says and then laughs. "I'm guessing it worked?"

"You knew about this?"

She nods.

"And you still came? Where are you sitting?"

"Tate's girlfriend Maggie is saving me a seat."

"The girlfriend section, really? I never."

Vivian rolls her eyes. "It's one game and I'm only here to support you."

"That's how it starts," I tell her. "Next thing you know, you're head over heels for a hockey player."

My gaze goes to the ice where the guys from Boston are coming out for warm-ups. "I have to go. Wish me luck."

"Good luck," she calls after me.

I hurry down and take my place in the tunnel. The guys are vibrating with excitement and anticipation. Lex shifts from foot to foot, eyes straight ahead.

"All right, boys. Everybody ready?" Coach Garfunkle asks.

A series of cheers and grunts echo from the group of guys. My guys.

I watch them pass by, inspecting their gear and then running through my checklist. I follow them out and then double-check the bench.

"Stand still, Dalager, you're making me nervous," Coach Keller says. He loosens his tie.

"Sorry. I keep thinking I forgot something."

He scans the bench. "Looks good. Try to relax. We're going to need you to stay loose and ready." Then he winks. Maybe Coach Keller has a soft side after all.

"Kirk, what in God's green earth are you doing? Get out there and warm up," Coach growls at our goalie.

Then again, maybe not.

Good things, like bad, seem to come in pairs. Lex not only gets a chance to play with the second line, he scores the game-winning goal.

We head to the Biscuit after the game. I don't bother changing out of my new hockey jersey. I guess I'm one of them now. At their usual table, I sit in a chair wedged in next to Lex, and someone pushes a beer in front of me.

He drapes an arm around my shoulders as he accepts congrats from the server on his goal tonight. "Thanks, I had my lucky charm."

My stomach flutters as he winks at me. "What'd I tell you about luck?"

"That I hold my own." He wraps both arms around me. "Get it? Hold my own?"

"Oh brother," Patrick groans. "This the kind of shit we have to look forward to? I need new friends."

"At least you don't have to live with him," Ash says. "I need to find someone to help me drown out the noise of you two." He sits tall and looks around the tables. Two girls are vying for spots on his lap before he's done a full sweep of the place.

"As easy as snapping your fingers." I roll my eyes.

"Where's Vivian tonight?" Lex asks. "I was kind of looking forward to seeing her sitting around a table of hockey players."

"She wouldn't be caught dead at this table."

"Look who's talking." He pulls on my jersey and drops a kiss to my lips.

"Vonne," someone calls his name and reluctantly I break the kiss. This is his night. He should enjoy every second of the attention.

And he's good at taking the praise. Humble and appreciative.

"Looks like he finally got what he wanted," Pax says with a nudge from my other side. "Rookie gets to talk about his hockey game all night."

"I heard that," Lex says, leaning around me. He hasn't stopped touching me, even as he's been pulled in a million different conversations.

"You earned it," Pax says and lifts his glass to him.

"Thanks, man. I appreciate it." Lex looks to me. "Are you bored to tears? Do you want to leave?"

"And miss out on everyone talking about how great my boyfriend is? Fat chance."

We close down the place. The guys start to grab sober rides, but Lex and I decide to walk back.

"I really need to get a fucking coat," he says, holding my hand and hurrying down the sidewalk.

I'm dressed appropriately with a hat, scarf, and gloves, and I'm still cold.

"Here." I unravel my scarf and then he humors me by letting me wrap it around his neck. "Pink is a good color on you."

"Yeah?"

"And I didn't realize what good leverage it provides." I yank on one end, forcing him to step into me.

His face is cold as I go up on my toes to kiss him. Icy hands work their way into my coat and under my shirt. I inhale sharply as his frozen fingers zap the warmth from my heated skin.

"I will so get you back for this." I can barely form words from the shock of cold.

"Come on, baby doll. I know just what to do. We need to get naked and lie together so we can share body heat and warm you up."

"Oh how selfless of you."

He nods with a big, boyish grin. Warmth spreads through my insides, though, so ridiculous but effective.

We barely make it into his room before he's stripping me out of my layers and kissing me like it's been months instead of hours since we've had sex. Being the focus of Lex's attention still trips me up. There aren't any doubts in the way he touches me. All in. And for once, I give it back the same way. No hesitation. I might crash and burn, but not without someone waiting to pick me back up.

"What time is your alarm set for?" I ask him as he picks me up and carries me toward the bed. "I was planning on going to the rink early tomorrow. I didn't finish all the laundry."

"No alarm." He takes my mouth again and I lose myself to his taste and the hungry way he consumes me with every stroke of his tongue.

I have to push at his chest to get a word in. "What do you mean, no alarm? Aren't you getting up to run?"

"Nope." He grins. "Thought I'd sleep in tomorrow."

"I see. Now that you've made it, you're gonna start slacking," I joke.

He runs a finger along my jaw and tips my chin up to meet his lips. "Turns out, some things are more important than hockey."

26

LEX

It's New Year's Eve eve, but we're partying tonight because we have a game on the first. Tomorrow night I'll be tucked in early and miss the start of a new year. Not all bad since I'll have my girl with me. The new year is already looking up.

Kaitlyn is supervising the twins as they move the living room furniture around to make room for dancing.

"A little more to the right," she says. Hands on hips, she watches as they carry our ancient and heavy couch to the far wall. "No, I think I liked it back over there."

"Tell me why we're rearranging the entire first floor again?" Ash asks as he stands beside me. "No one's ever complained about the setup before."

"Kaitlyn thinks we need a place for dancing."

He raises a brow and crosses his arms over his chest. "You are so fucked."

"Yep." No reason in denying it. I'm a goner. If she asked to paint the walls pink and add a reading nook, I'd probably be at the home good store picking out color swatches. "Vivian's stopping by. I hear she likes to dance."

"I don't think I'll be doing any dancing. It still hurts to walk."

"Guess that also rules out sex."

My buddy took a nasty hit and injured his groin in last weekend's game. He's out for at least another two weeks.

"I never rule out sex." He chuckles and then winces. "Fuck. I need to go sit down."

Kaitlyn bounds over with a big grin as Ash hobbles off. "What do you think?"

"You look perfect." She really does. The silver dress she's wearing is short and silky. Her boots come up over her knees and boost her up a few inches so that her lips are closer to my level.

"I meant the house." She grins at me with those killer lips coated in red. Yep, that's gonna be all over me tonight.

"Oh yeah, also perfect."

"I know you're just saying that, but I don't even care. Tonight is going to be amazing." She wraps her arms around my neck. "I've never kissed anyone that I actually liked on New Year's Eve."

"New Year's Eve eve."

"Same difference. We're going to do a mock ball drop, complete with champagne. Vivian splurged on the good stuff."

"She knows that the party is here, right? At a house full of hockey dudes?"

"Yes. She's just choosing to overlook it."

I chuckle. "Well, Ash is out of commission for a while so he's basically not a hockey player."

"I doubt she'll see it that way. It's like in your blood or something. Once a hockey player, always a hockey player."

"You say it like we're contagious."

She hums a teasing response.

An hour later, my house is filled way beyond capacity. The

party is loud and crazy. The dance floor is a big hit. Girls are dancing, holding drinks and spilling them on our hardwood floors. That'll be a pain to clean up.

Kaitlyn is in the middle of it all. I'm not sure I've ever seen her having so much fun. Makes the thought of mopping floors tomorrow a little more bearable.

Me and the guys are standing around, holding up the walls, and watching.

"I miss having somewhere to sit," Pax says as he shifts his weight from one leg to the other.

"There's room on the end of the couch," I say and motion toward it. On the opposite end, a petite redhead is straddling Kirk and he's got his hands up the front of her shirt.

"Yeah, no thanks. I think you might need to burn that thing after tonight."

Not a terrible idea. It's definitely going to take a few days to burn the image from my brain. I think I'll be sitting on the floor from now on.

"Do you want to play washers outside or… anything but stand here?"

"No. I think I've gotta go in the belly of the beast," I say. Kaitlyn is beckoning me from the center of the dance floor with a sexy smile that I can't resist.

"Good luck with that." Pax laughs as I step toward her.

Arms flailing, hips shaking—the mass of girls dancing in my living room is sort of terrifying as I get close. I've watched more than one girl enter and get sucked into the vortex. Luckily, Kaitlyn meets me at the edge of the crowd. "Dance with me?"

"Later." And by later I mean alone in my room, very naked. "I have a surprise for you."

"Mmm. Me too." Her lips brush against mine and her arms go around my neck. She's flush against me and still swaying side to side. Dancing like this isn't so bad. Actually, there aren't a lot of things I couldn't endure while kissing Kaitlyn.

It's been like that from day one. She just does something for me that I can't describe. Being near her is a rush. Kissing her is a high. Loving her is the best feeling in the world.

She pulls back and then brings a thumb to my lower lip. "Sorry."

"You got it all over me, didn't you?"

"It's a good shade for you. What was your surprise?"

I pull the Sharpie from my pocket.

"A marker?" She takes it from my hand. "Are we going to wait until people pass out and draw dicks on their faces?"

"What? No." I laugh. "And damn, remind me to get that back when we're done."

I lead her into the dining room to the table that holds generations of hockey players' signatures. "It's time to make our mark."

"Our?"

"All the past equipment managers are on here too." I point to Alec's name and then the guy that was here before him.

"Where should I sign?" she asks with a giddy grin.

"Anywhere you want. It doesn't matter."

"Says the guy who's been putting off signing all year."

"Ladies first, of course."

She's smiling as she takes the Sharpie and scrawls her name on the table. And I'm smiling too as I write mine beside hers. I finally figured out where it belongs, where *I* belong. Here, next to her.

"We did it." I slide my arm around her waist. I swear it gives me chills looking at my name on this epic piece of history.

"Now what?"

"First, a summer together in Boston, a couple more years of

school, then you'll be a badass marketing boss, and I'll be a big shot hockey star." I like the image as I speak it out loud.

Kaitlyn turned down the internship at Hawthorne and is working for her dad this summer. You could have knocked me over with a feather when she told me, but I'm excited for her. I'm looking forward to her showing me around the city and just spending more time with her. The first summer of many, hopefully.

"I meant tonight, weirdo."

"Oh. Well, that's easy. Let's go party with our friends."

And that's exactly what we do.

THE
END

Made in the USA
Columbia, SC
13 May 2021